AVENGERS®

The Ultimate Guide

Tom DeFalco

MARVEL

DK

Contents

Foreword by Stan Lee

It had to happen.

They were too mighty, too powerful, too popular! Every comic book fan had the same demand: "You must team them up! You must let them become Earth's Mightiest Team!"

Well, you know us. Your wish is our command. And so the Avengers was born.

In the beginning, we started slowly. Our first Avengers lineup consisted of Thor, Iron Man, Ant Man/Giant Man and the wondrous Wasp. But we couldn't wait to see the fireworks that would ensue if we added the Hulk and Sub-Mariner. And, of course, tossing in Captain America to lead the team was a no-brainer.

I loved the idea of having Iron Man's Fifth Avenue mansion become their headquarters. You wouldn't believe how many Marvel Comics fans, upon visiting New York, would immediately head for Fifth Avenue, desperately trying to find the mansion, hoping to get a glimpse of one of the Avengers, just as I used to search Baker Street when I visited London, certain I'd run into Sherlock Holmes and Dr. Watson sooner or later.

Of course, as time went by, some Avengers temporarily left the team while others were added. In fact, after the first few months, I had to keep referring to a list on my desk telling me who was a member at any given time because I couldn't keep track of them.

I guess almost every Marvel hero has been an Avenger at some time or other, but how about those great villains! Any team that has to fight the likes of Baron Zemo and his Masters of Evil, or Ultron, or Doctor Doom, or Kang the Conqueror, or the Mandarin, or Attuma, or Magneto—hey, you get the idea.

Of course, it was always fun to make good guys out of bad guys and vice versa, as in the case of Quicksilver and the Scarlet Witch. But I got the biggest kick out of the times when the group wouldn't be able to agree on who the next leader should be.

The thing is, when you run down the roster of Marvel's top heroes you've gotta realize it isn't an easy choice!

We certainly weren't bashful about including the fair sex, either. Who can forget the beautiful and exotic Enchantress, the Black Widow, Hellcat, Ms. Marvel, Tigra, Spider-Woman, Morgan Le Fey, Crystal, She-Hulk and the many other scintillating female characters whose fans will hate me because I forgot to mention them here. But, even though I may have forgotten a few, there's no way *you'll* forget them because you'll soon be feasting your eyes on each and every one on the *pandemonious* pages that follow!

One of the more interesting things about the Avengers is that every decade or so we get a whole new take on Earth's mightiest team. The original Avengers of the 1960s gave way to the new and different ones of the 1970s who, in turn, morphed into the Avengers of the 1980s. This team then transformed itself in the 1990s, until finally we have the new and exciting group that Marvel has gifted us with today.

But no matter how eloquently I describe the grandeur and glory of the Avengers, I can't begin to do justice to the wonderment you'll find in this book. So settle back and let your love of fantasy and adventure savor the magic and mystique of Earth's Mightiest Hero Team.

Excelsior!

Stan Lee

FATEFUL DISCOVERY

Odin disguised Thor's magic hammer as an old walking stick and hid it in a cave, knowing that his son would find it one day.

THOR

NO ONE EVER SAID that being a god would be easy... Mighty Thor is a member of a virtually immortal race of superhuman beings who were once worshiped as the Norse Gods. The son of Odin, lord of Asgard, Thor was raised to be a courageous warrior and a compassionate monarch. He battled the enemies of Asgard and performed amazing feats of valor and nobility. But as his accomplishments grew, so did his ego.

THE CAVE IS BATHED IN BLINDING LIGHT!! LIKE A FIERY BOLT OF LIGHTNING! AND THE ANCIENT CAN--IT--*IT'S CHANGING SHAPE!*

AND-- *I'M CHANGING TOO!!*

CAN THIS BE REALLY *HAPPENING* --OR AM I GOING *MAD?!!*

HEALER AND HERO

To teach his headstrong son humility, Odin stripped Thor of his memory and sent him to Earth in the mortal guise of a lame medical student named Donald Blake. As Blake, Thor learned to care for the sick and dying. He eventually became a successful physician and surgeon.

THOR'S HAMMER

Thor's enchanted hammer, Mjolnir, is virtually indestructible and can only be lifted by someone who is worthy of the thunder god's power.

NO! IT *ISN'T* MAD!! I CAN FEEL MY BODY BURSTING WITH *POWER*-- POWER SUCH AS I'VE NEVER KNOWN!!

Earth's Protector

After being exiled for nearly ten years, Thor regained his magic hammer and his power, but Odin had done his work too well. Thor had grown to love humankind. Determined to protect the Earth, he became a founder member of the Avengers.

THE *TEEN BRIGADE!* THEY'RE LOCATED IN THE SOUTH-WEST! IF THIS CONCERNS THE *HULK*, IT MUST BE SERIOUS! AND SO, THE TIME HAS COME...

...FOR DR. DON BLAKE TO STRIKE HIS ENCHANTED CANE ONCE UPON THE FLOOR, CASTING OFF HIS MORTAL GUISE, AND BECOMING...

...THE MIGHTY *THOR*, GOD OF *THUNDER!*

Call to Action

Thor is indirectly responsible for the formation of the Avengers. His half-brother Loki used the Hulk to lure Thor into a trap. When the Teen Brigade tried to contact the Fantastic Four, Loki redirected their radio signal so that Don Blake heard it and responded.

Asgard, Home of the Gods

The Asgardians were worshiped centuries ago by the Vikings. Odin is the ruler of Asgard and possesses vast powers. Other Asgardians include Heimdall, guardian of the Rainbow Bridge—a dimensional gateway linking Earth to Asgard—and Thor's friends Balder the brave, Hogun the grim, Fandral the dashing and the vainglorious Volstagg. After learning his true heritage, Donald Blake spent more of his time as Thor. However he has assumed other human identities over the years such as Sigurd Jarlson and Jake Olson.

YES, THAT WAS HOW IT *BEGAN!*

AND, FROM THAT TIME ONWARD, THE LIFE OF *DONALD BLAKE* WAS DESTINED TO NEVER BE THE *SAME!*

EACH PASSING *HOUR* BROUGHT NEW *WONDER...* NEW HIGH *ADVENTURE!*

THIS IS *LOKI,* MY ARCH-ENEMY! IT WAS *HE* WHO PLANNED THE TRAIN WRECK! IT WAS *HE* WHO ARRANGED FOR THE *HULK* TO BE BLAMED! ...IN ORDER TO MAKE *ME* APPEAR, SO THAT HE COULD TRAP ME!

IT WOULD SEEM THAT HE TRAPPED *HIMSELF!*

LOKI, HUH? *YOU* GOT ME INTO THIS JAM! LET ME *HAVE* 'IM, THOR!

BETA RAY BILL

Beta Ray Bill was the cyborg guardian of an alien race whose galaxy had been destroyed. He battled Thor and proved worthy to lift Mjolnir. Odin later gave Bill his own enchanted hammer.

Wizard of Lies

Loki is the Asgardian god of mischief and evil. Adopted by Odin after his Frost Giant father was killed in battle, he was raised as Thor's half-brother. Loki resented the Thunder God and vowed to destroy him. Loki is a shape-changer and a master of black magic, able to bring inanimate objects to life or endow anyone with superpowers. He can project himself through time and space and materialize wherever he likes. Loki hates the fact that his own misdeeds created the Avengers and will try anything to defeat them.

THUNDERSTRIKE

Eric Masterson was an architect who was briefly bonded with Thor and even took his place on the Avengers. Awarded his own magic mace, Thunderstrike was killed in combat.

Lady Sif

The sister of Heimdall, Sif was one of Thor's childhood playmates and she fell in love with him when they were teenagers. While she was training to be a warrior goddess, Thor was exiled to Earth and Donald Blake fell in love with Jane Foster, his nurse. After Thor regained his memory and broke up with his mortal girlfriend, he remembered the Lady Sif.

IRON MAN

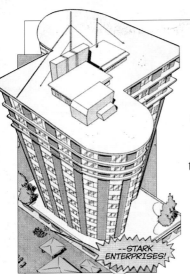

Corporate headquarters for Stark Industries.

TONY STARK, alias the super hero Iron Man, is one of the founders of the Avengers. Acting upon the Teen Brigade's plea for help to stop the rampaging Hulk, the wealthy industrialist donned his battle armor. In company with Ant-Man and the Wasp, he tracked down the Hulk and challenged him. Stark also donated the mansion that became the team's headquarters. He set up a trust fund to cover expenses and provided technical support and weaponry, including the Quinjets.

THE BOY GENIUS

Anthony "Tony" Stark had always believed in the power of technology to improve people's quality of life. The millionaire's son enrolled in an electrical engineering program at the Massachusetts Institute of Technology at the age of 15 and graduated at the top of his class. He inherited Stark Industries when he was only 21 and began designing and manufacturing high-tech weaponry for the government. Profits rose sharply under Tony's leadership and Stark Industries soon became one of the nation's leading industrial manufacturing complexes.

Stark can control his battle armor with a remote headset that transmits his mental commands.

LOOK! THERE'S TONY STARK!

UMMMNN... HE'S THE DREAMIEST THING THIS SIDE OF ROCK HUDSON!

THE RIVIERA WAS A REAL DRAG TILL *YOU* SHOWED UP, DARLING!

YES, ANTHONY STARK IS BOTH A SOPHISTIC AND A SCIENTIST! A MILLIONAIRE BACHELOR, AS MUCH AT HOME IN A LABORATORY AS IN HIGH SOCIETY!

Wine and Roses

Tony Stark enjoyed the good life. He was rich and handsome. His address book contained the private numbers of movie stars and supermodels. He knew how to make money and was even better at spending it. However, Tony also took his work seriously. He was constantly inventing new technologies or improving old ones.

The Iron Man armor contains weapons such as laser cannons, magnetic field generators, concussion blasters, flamethrowers, and mini-missile launchers.

AND, TRIPPING OVER A SMALL, CONCEALED STRING LEADS TO DISASTER...

BAROOM

A BOOBY-TRAP! OHHH...

A Matter of Life and Death

While testing an invention in Southeast Asia, a jungle booby trap exploded and shrapnel lodged near his heart. Tony was captured by the Warlord, who ordered him to construct a super-weapon. Knowing that it was only a matter of time before the shrapnel killed him, he built an armored suit with another prisoner. The armored chest plate kept his heart beating and give him superhuman strength.

Stark later painted his armor gold at the suggestion of one of his lady friends.

AND THEN, WHEN THE DOOMED AMERICAN'S CONDITION BE-COMES CRITICAL -- WHEN HE CAN NO LONGER STAND...

THE LIFE-GIVING HEART OF YOUR IRON BODY IS *READY!* QUICKLY...CLAMP IT AROUND YOUR CHEST!

The Golden Avenger

Tony used his new Iron Man armor to escape the Warlord and return to the U.S. Tony wore his armored chest plate beneath his clothes for years, but no longer needs it to survive. Since Iron Man was often seen at Stark Industries, Tony circulated the story that " The Golden Avenger" was his personal bodyguard.

War Machine

While acting as Iron Man, Rhodes battled enemies such as the Radioactive Man, the Mandarin, and the Zodiac. He even became one of the first members of the West Coast Avengers. When Stark reassumed his Iron Man role, he replaced Rhodes on the Avengers. Stark later gave Rhodes his own suit of armor. The War Machine battlesuit had its own air supply and enabled flight or underwater travel. Its exoskeleton made Rhodes almost as strong as Thor. Its weaponry included repulsor rays, tractor beams, and an electromagnetic pulse generator. The suit also came with a shoulder-mounted micro-rocket launcher, a pair of gatling guns and a wrist-mounted laser blade.

THE WEST COASTER

Leaving Stark's employ, Rhodes was a member of the West Coast Avengers until the team disbanded. War Machine is still active and continues to fight crime on the West Coast.

SUITED UP

Tony Stark is constantly making adjustments to his suit of armor or building suits that have specific uses or weaponry. He stores nearly a hundred fully functioning suits, but is still building more.

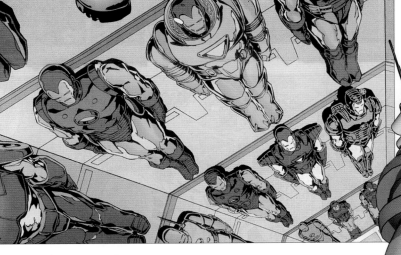

HOWEVER, THE RECHARGING CONNECTIONS HAD BEEN JURY-RIGGED IN TIME, AND AS THE LAST WATTS OF ELECTRICITY HAD BEEN DRAINED FROM THE HELICOPTER'S BATTERIES...

THANKS, LIEUTENANT. I NEEDED THAT.

UH. DON'T MENTION IT.

A Friend in Need

James Rhodes was a Marine pilot stationed in Southeast Asia. Shot out of the sky, he was trying to fix his helicopter when Iron Man walked out of the jungle. Having just escaped the Warlord, Stark was trying to make his way back to American lines. Though the helicopter could not be repaired, its batteries recharged Iron Man's power supply. The two men became friends as they crossed the jungle to safety and Rhodes became Stark's pilot and confidant. When personal problems forced Stark to temporarily give up being Iron Man, he asked "Rhodey" to assume the responsibility.

NEVERTHELESS, YOU'RE A GOOD MAN. IF I EVER REQUIRE THE SERVICES OF A PILOT WHILE I'M HERE, I HOPE YOU'LL BE AVAILABLE.

AND IF YOU NEED A JOB WHEN THESE HOSTILITIES ARE OVER, PLEASE DON'T HESITATE TO GIVE ME A CALL.

HENRY PYM

ANT-MAN
1962

DR. HENRY "HANK" PYM was a brilliant biochemist who developed a formula that made use of subatomic elements that he dubbed "Pym particles." These particles could shrink and enlarge the size of any object. He tested the formula on himself and shrunk himself to the size of an ant! After regaining his normal height and weight, the relieved Pym poured the rest of his formula down the sink.

Inside the Ant Hill

When Pym first shrank to ant size, he stumbled outside and was attacked by worker ants. Seeking refuge in an nearby ant hill, he became mired in a honey-filled tunnel. Fortunately, a friendly ant pulled him to safety and took him back home.

TALKING TO INSECTS

Pym came to regret his hasty action and recreated the formula. Haunted by the death of his first wife, a foreign dissident murdered by her government's secret police, he resolved to use his formula to fight for justice. He spent the next few months studying ants and built a cybernetic helmet that enabled him to communicate with them.

AN INSTANT LATER, THE POWERFUL INSECT STRIKES...

BUT TO HIS SURPRISE, HENRY PYM IS ABLE TO LIFT HIS LARGE ADVERSARY INTO THE AIR...

HUMAN POWER

While reduced to ant-sized, Pym still possessed the strength of a full-grown man. He was also a skilled fighter.

GIANT MAN
1963

Giant-Man rushes to the Mansion to get medical treatment for the Wasp.

BIG IDEAS

Pym became partners with the Wasp and they joined the Avengers. A few months later, he adapted his formula to increase his size and power as Giant-Man.

WHAT...?! WHAT IN THE NAME OF CREATION IS *THAT*??!

JUST MADE IT! ANOTHER MINUTE AND I'D HAVE BEEN *CRUSHED* INSIDE THOSE WALLS!

HAH! NOW I'LL FINISH YOU OFF WITH MY WEBBING, AND THEN... HEY! *WHAT* --- ??

I'LL ADMIT YOU MADE A PRETTY GOOD SHOWING AGAINST *ANT-MAN*, FELLA!...

...BUT *NOW*, LET'S SEE HOW YOU RATE AGAINST HIS OVER-SIZED ALTER-EGO... BETTER KNOWN TO THE LIKES OF YOU AS... *GIANT-MAN!*

ATTA BOY, HIGH-POCKETS! GO *GET* HIM! MAKE SPIDER STEW OUT OF HIM!

SIZE MATTERS

Giant-Man usually stood 10 feet (3 meters) tall, although he could attain 25 feet (7.6 meters) in height. His strength grew in direct proportion to his height, but so did the strain on his body. Growing to gigantic size always left him physically exhausted.

GIANT-MAN
1965

THE WASP'S IN DANGER!

CUTAWAY DIAGRAM OF WAFER-THIN CYBERNETIC HELMET

Pym's cybernetic helmet allows him to communicate and control ants and higher insects.

Among Us Walks a Goliath

After taking a small leave of absence, Pym returned to the Avengers with a new costume and new name. But Goliath strained himself and became trapped at giant size for many months.

THAT'S THE BEST OFFER I'VE HAD ALL DAY -- - MMMM! - THIS IS LIKE OLD TIMES -- AND I *LOVE* IT!

OHHH!

HANK! WHAT IS IT? WHAT'S *WRONG*!?

I WAS *CARELESS*! I REMAINED GIANT-SIZED *TOO LONG*! NOW THE SUDDEN STRAIN OF *SHRINKING* IS TOO MUCH!

HANK!

HE *STOPPED* SHRINKING -- AT *TEN FEET*! HE NEVER DID IT BEFORE! HE'S *BLACKING OUT*!

CAN'T *CONTROL* IT ANY LONGER...! IF -- IF I DON'T GET MY ABILITY *BACK* -- I'LL *REMAIN* THIS WAY -- TEN FEET TALL -- FOREVER! *FOREVER*! OHHH --!

IS HE -- IS HE -- ?

HE'S STILL BREATHING! BUT -- IF HE LOST HIS POWER TO CHANGE SIZE THAT MEANS HE'LL REMAIN *TEN FEET* TALL! HE'LL BE -- A *FREAK*!

I GRIEVE FOR HIM!

IT'S *MY* FAULT! HE DID IT TO SAVE *ME* -- AND NOW -- LOOK WHAT I'VE *DONE* TO HIM!

DON'T REPROACH YOURSELF JAN! HE'D GIVE HIS LIFE A *HUNDRED* TIMES TO SAVE YOURS!

BUT CAN IT BE THAT *ANOTHER* AVENGER HAS LEFT OUR RANKS -- TO RETURN *NO MORE*!!

TRADING NAMES

Pym is the first costumed adventurer to call himself Goliath; Clint Barton and Bill Foster also used the name and powers for a brief time. Erik Josten, who began as the villainous Power Man, then took the name, before calling himself Atlas.

The Haunted Hero

With the aid of Dr. Bill Foster, who would later become another Giant-Man, Pym regained his normal size. A series of disappointments, failures, and tragedies plagued Pym and he suffered a series of mental breakdowns.

GOLIATH 1969

YELLOWJACKET

While suffering from a split personality, Pym created another new costumed identity, an aggressive, arrogant hero called Yellowjacket. He and the Wasp finally married but did not live happily ever after.

GIANT-MAN 2000

As Giant-Man, Pym can now reach a top height of 100 feet tall (30.4 meters)

OUT OF MY WAY! *NOTHING'S* STOPPING ME FROM REACHING THAT FLAME -- *NOTHING*!

FOR ALL HIS TITANIC *SIZE*, HE MOVES WITH THE SPEED OF A *CYCLONE*!

CRAK!

YELLOWJACKET 1968

A Team Player

Pym's mental problems grew, and his marriage to the Wasp ended in divorce. He tried to retire from costumed heroics, but later served as the resident scientist for the West Coast Avengers. No matter how many times he tries to quit, Henry Pym always returns to the Avengers.

A FAMILIAR FACE

They looked strikingly similar, but Janet's sunny disposition was the complete opposite of Henry Pym's former wife.

The WASP

JANET VAN DYNE was the daughter of well known scientist Vernon van Dyne. He planned to use a beam of gamma radiation to detect intelligent life on other planets and tried to interest Dr. Henry Pym in the project. Janet found herself attracted to Pym, who was also drawn to her, seeing a resemblance between Janet and his late wife. Pym decided not to work on the experiment, but Vernon proceeded without him and discovered a planet inhabited by an alien race, the Kosmosians.

CELLULAR SURGERY

Pym implanted cells beneath Janet's skin at her shoulder blades and temples, so that she could grow wings and antennae whenever she shrank to insect size.

ALIEN KILLER

Pilai, a criminal from Kosmos, used van Dyne's beam to teleport himself to Earth and murdered the scientist. Janet discovered her father's body and immediately called Pym. After learning that Janet wanted to bring the killer to justice and protect other innocent people from harm, Pym revealed that he was Ant-Man and invited her to become a costumed crime-fighter. She immediately accepted and he gave her the ability to become the Wasp.

Ant-Man and the Wasp soon tracked down the murderous Pilai and defeated him.

Staying Together

Ant-Man and the Wasp continued to work together and soon fell in love. They became founding members of the Avengers, joining in many early battles with the Hulk, Sub-Mariner, Baron Zemo, and Kang. In time, however, Pym wanted to return to his scientific research work; he decided to retire from crime-fighting and Janet joined him.

WIT OF THE WASP WOMAN

Confident and independent, Janet knows that men find her attractive and she likes to flirt. Her fun-loving personality can make her seem shallow, but her mind is razor-sharp.

Adventurous Spirit

Unlike Pym, Janet loved being the Wasp and tried to lure him back into costume. She also went on solo adventures, using her size-changing powers and scientific knowledge that she had picked up from Pym.

I STILL HAVE **ONE** THING IN MY FAVOR--

THEY DON'T SUSPECT THAT THEY'VE CAPTURED THE **WASP** -- A HUMAN WHO CAN INSTANTLY BECOME **INSECT-SIZED!**

I'VE GOT TO HOLD MY BREATH FOR THE NEXT FEW MINUTES -- NO MATTER **WHAT!**

THANK HEAVENS HANK USED TO SPEND TIME TEACHING ME THE FUNDAMENTALS OF ELECTRO-COMMUNICATIONS!

OTHERWISE, I MIGHT NEVER HAVE **RECOGNIZED** THIS APPARATUS AS A MODIFIED SHORT-WAVE TRANSMITTER! -- OR, EVEN RECOGNIZING IT, I WOULDN'T HAVE KNOWN WHAT TO **DO!**

The Wasp has her "wasp stings"—bio-electric force bolts she can project from her hands.

Pym modified Janet's body so that she actually gains strength as she shrinks.

Janet briefly used Pym's growth formula to become Giant-Girl, but preferred being the Wasp.

--THERE'S A WHOLE **WORLD** OF **CULTURE** TO EXPLORE.

DIFFERENT **LANGUAGES** AND **FOODS.**

RELIGIONS AND **CUSTOMS.**

The Wasp can increase or decrease her size at will.

A Rocky Relationship

After inheriting her father's fortune, Janet embarked on a career as a fashion designer. She enjoyed the good things of life and creating new costumes for herself. She and Pym married, but, sadly, his deteriorating mental condition drove them apart. He resigned from the Avengers, but she stayed with the team.

Always an Avenger

The Wasp eventually became the Avengers' first female chairperson. She served two terms and proved to be almost as good at combat strategy as Captain America. She moved to California and worked with the West Coast team for a while, but currently lives in the New York area.

15

LOOK! THAT HEAD JUTTING THROUGH THE TRACKS!

IT'S THE *HULK!* HE DID THIS! HE'S TRYING TO KILL US ALL! I--I CAN'T STOP IN TIME!

EMERGENCY STOP
Trickster Loki made Hulk believe there was dynamite on the tracks.

The AVENGERS' ORIGIN

IMPRISONED ON the dreaded Isle of Silence for crimes against Thor, Loki planned his revenge on the thunder god. He projected his consciousness to the Earth and began searching for a menace powerful enough to challenge his hated half-brother. He soon spotted the incredible Hulk and tricked him into destroying a train trestle. When Rick Jones heard about the Hulk's rampage, he summoned the members of his newly formed Teen Brigade and attempted to contact the Fantastic Four.

CALL TO ACTION

The Teen Brigade used a homemade radio to reach the Fantastic Four. However, Loki didn't want them involved and he diverted the signal so that Dr. Donald Blake heard the cry for help. Blake immediately transformed into the mighty Thor. The astonishing Ant-Man and the wondrous Wasp also responded… and so did the invincible Iron Man!

THEN, THE ONE LIVING BEING WHO KNOWS THE TRUTH ABOUT THE HULK READS THE REPORT IN AMAZEMENT!

IT *CAN'T* BE! HE'D *NEVER* DO A THING LIKE THAT!.. NO MATTER *WHAT!!*

OR..OR *WOULD* HE?

TRAIN ENGINEER IDENTIFIES HULK AS WOULD-BE WRECKER!

HEADLINE NEWS
Whether the Hulk was innocent or guilty of wrecking the railroad, Rick knew only the Fantastic Four could stop him.

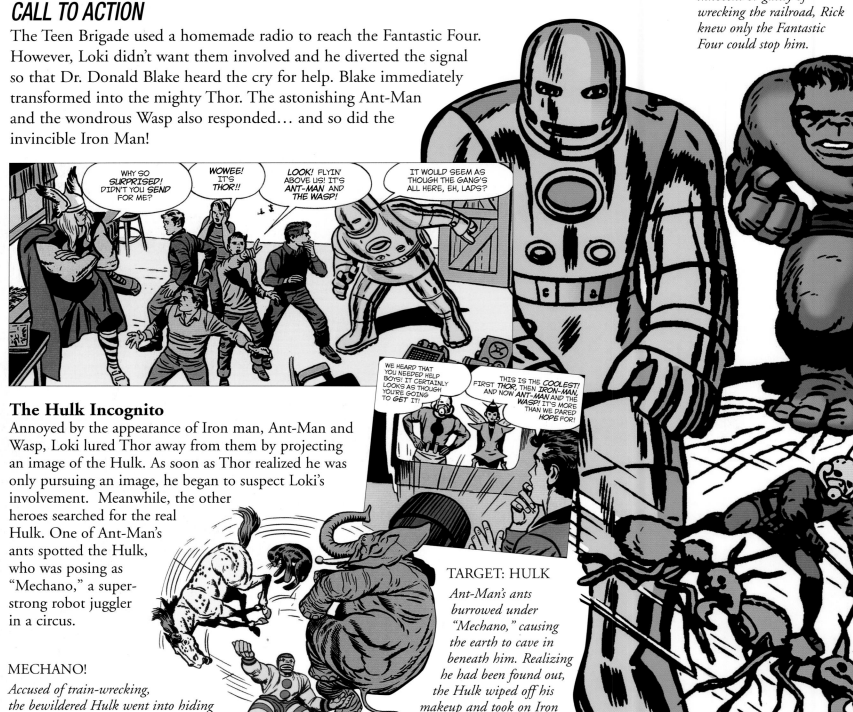

WHY SO *SURPRISED!* DIDN'T YOU *SEND* FOR ME?

WOWEE! IT'S *THOR!!*

LOOK! FLYIN' ABOVE US! IT'S *ANT-MAN* AND *THE WASP!*

IT WOULD SEEM AS THOUGH THE GANG'S ALL HERE, EH, LADS?

WE HEARD THAT YOU NEEDED HELP BOYS! IT CERTAINLY LOOKS AS THOUGH YOU'RE GOING TO *GET* IT!

THIS IS THE *COOLEST!* FIRST *THOR,* THEN *IRON-MAN,* AND NOW *ANT-MAN* AND THE *WASP!* IT'S MORE THAN WE DARED *HOPE* FOR!

The Hulk Incognito
Annoyed by the appearance of Iron man, Ant-Man and Wasp, Loki lured Thor away from them by projecting an image of the Hulk. As soon as Thor realized he was only pursuing an image, he began to suspect Loki's involvement. Meanwhile, the other heroes searched for the real Hulk. One of Ant-Man's ants spotted the Hulk, who was posing as "Mechano," a super-strong robot juggler in a circus.

MECHANO!
Accused of train-wrecking, the bewildered Hulk went into hiding as Mechano, "The Marvel of the Age."

TARGET: HULK
Ant-Man's ants burrowed under "Mechano," causing the earth to cave in beneath him. Realizing he had been found out, the Hulk wiped off his makeup and took on Iron Man, Ant-Man, and Wasp.

The Glowing God
Thor raced back to Earth with proof that the Hulk was innocent. Undeterred, Loki cast a spell that made his body radioactive and prepared to battle the thunder god. However, a horde of ants swarmed over a switch—and sent Loki tumbling into a lead-lined tank.

TEAM BUILDING
With Loki out of the way, the heroes realized their powers could be complimentary.

Avengers Assemble!
Ant-Man suggested that the heroes form a team to fight foes and menaces that were too powerful for a single hero. Sick of being hunted and hounded, even the Hulk agreed to join… and thus were the Avengers Assembled!

Teen Brigade

The Teen Brigade was a loose-knit group of young, amateur radio enthusiasts who originally banded together to keep track of the Hulk's movements. The team often came to the aid of the Avengers and even managed to free them when they were taken prisoner by Kang.

Rick Jones

Rick was a teenage orphan who, acting on a dare, drove onto a bomb test site and caused Dr. Bruce Banner to be exposed to gamma radiation and become the Hulk. Feeling guilty, Rick often helped both Banner and the Hulk. After the Hulk quit the Avengers, Rick stayed with the team as an unofficial member. He eventually merged with the original Captain Marvel, and later his son.

The MANSION

AVENGERS MANSION was originally built in 1932 to house the Stark family. Located at 890 Fifth Avenue in Manhattan, New York City, it is a three-story townhouse with three additional below-ground levels. The Mansion was donated to the Avengers by Tony Stark, one of the founding members, and has been significantly modified to fit the team's special needs. The above ground levels contain all the areas open to the public and the team's living quarters. The below-ground levels contain the team's classified equipment, weaponry, files, and computer systems.

EDWIN JARVIS

Stark set up a foundation to cover the team's expenses and the salary of loyal major domo Edwin Jarvis.

FAITHFUL SERVANT

Edwin Jarvis is a war hero and a former pilot in Britain's Royal Air Force who retired to the U.S. to become Tony Stark's butler. When Stark transferred ownership of his mansion to the Avengers, he asked Jarvis to stay on as the team's principal domestic servant. Jarvis has served the team ever since.

He supervises the staff, and is the only servant who lives in the mansion.

The foyer, main dining hall, public conference room, library, kitchen and Jarvis' quarters are all located on the Mansion's ground floor.

Top Security

Surrounded by a concrete wall 12 feet (3.65 meters) high and 1 ft (30 cm) thick, the Mansion is a virtual fortress. The walls, yard, doors, windows, and roof are wired with state-of-the-art surveillance equipment; no one can enter the grounds without being observed. A range of detainment devices sited around the property intercept unauthorized visitors. Stark personally reviews and upgrades the system each year.

The Quinjet hanger and landing dock is located on the Mansion's third floor.

SUPERSONIC POWER

Capable of vertical take-offs and landings, the Avengers' Quinjets can hover like a helicopter or fly at maximum speeds of Mach 2.1.

Eight master-bedroom suites and four guest rooms are available for any full-time Avenger who wishes to live at the Mansion.

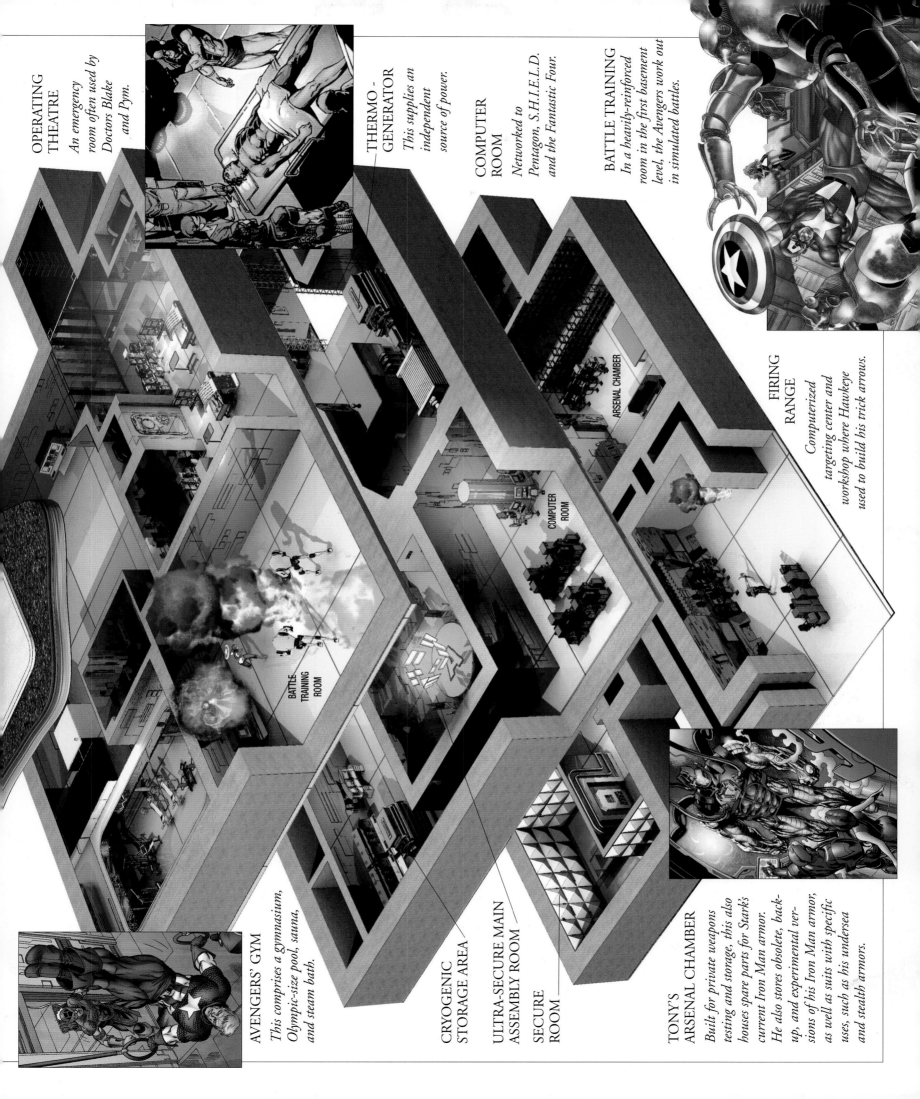

OPERATING THEATRE
An emergency room often used by Doctors Blake and Pym.

THERMO-GENERATOR
This supplies an independent source of power.

COMPUTER ROOM
Networked to Pentagon, S.H.I.E.L.D. and the Fantastic Four.

BATTLE TRAINING
In a heavily-reinforced room in the first basement level, the Avengers work out in simulated battles.

ARSENAL CHAMBER

COMPUTER ROOM

BATTLE-TRAINING ROOM

FIRING RANGE
Computerized targeting center and workshop where Hawkeye used to build his trick arrows.

AVENGERS' GYM
This comprises a gymnasium, Olympic-size pool, sauna, and steam bath.

CRYOGENIC STORAGE AREA

ULTRA-SECURE MAIN ASSEMBLY ROOM

SECURE ROOM

TONY'S ARSENAL CHAMBER
Built for private weapons testing and storage, this also houses spare parts for Stark's current Iron Man armor. He also stores obsolete, back-up, and experimental versions of his Iron Man armor, as well as suits with specific uses, such as his undersea and stealth armors.

THE AVENGERS IN THE 1960s

THE MARVEL UNIVERSE was only two years old when the Avengers first appeared. After creating the Fantastic Four with Jack Kirby in 1961, Stan Lee teamed up with Jack Kirby and artists Steve Ditko and Don Heck to create other super heroes like the Hulk, Spider-Man, Thor, Iron Man and Ant-Man. When the time came to launch a new title, it seemed natural to team up some of their current heroes. The Avengers weren't like any other super-team. Where the Fantastic Four was a family, the Avengers were a team of all-stars with an ever-changing roster. The group first gathered together to fight the Hulk and then invited him to become a member. He agreed, but only stayed for one issue. Captain America joined in the fourth issue and a whole new team was introduced in Avengers #16.

The creative team also underwent changes: Stan Lee and Jack Kirby began the series, but Jack left the title's interiors after only eight issues, although he continued drawing the covers for the next few years. Artist Don Heck took over in 1964 and penciled 22 issues and an annual. He was followed by John Buscema in 1967, who did about 21 issues. Gene Colan, Barry Windsor-Smith and Sal Buscema all succeeded John, producing a few issues each. Stan Lee scripted the first 34 issues and writer Roy Thomas took up the reins in 1966 with a run that continued into the 1970s.

The Avengers #4 (March, 1964) Captain America is resurrected from comics' Golden Age and joins the team. *(Cover by Jack Kirby and George Roussos)*

The Avengers Annual #1 (Sept. 1967) The Mandarin gathers a squad of super-villains to take on both the original members and the new Avengers team in a story by Roy Thomas and Don Heck. *(Cover by John Buscema and George Roussos)*

1963

The Avengers #1 (Sept. 1963) Earth's Mightiest Heroes assemble to combat Loki. *(Cover by Jack Kirby and Dick Ayers)*

1964

The Avengers #3 (Jan. 1964) The Hulk joins the Sub-Mariner against his former team. *(Cover by Jack Kirby and Paul Reinman)*

1965

The Avengers #16 (May 1965) A new group of Avengers takes over the title. *(Cover by Jack Kirby and Sol Brodsky)*

1966

The Avengers #30 (July 1966) The Avengers discover El Dorado. *(Cover by Jack Kirby and Frank Giacoia)*

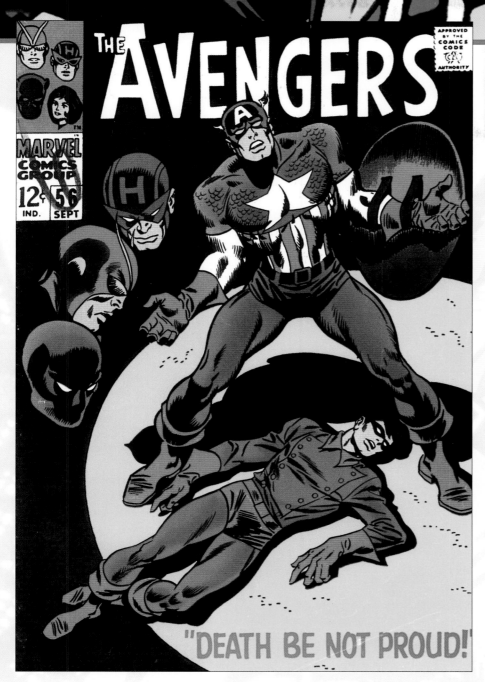

"DEATH BE NOT PROUD!"

The Avengers #63 (April 1969) Hawkeye exchanges his arrows for Hank Pym's growth serum and becomes the new Goliath. *(Cover by Gene Colan and George Klein)*

The Avengers #56 (Sept. 1968) Captain America relives the death of his partner, Bucky Barnes. *(Cover by John Buscema and George Klein)*

1967   **1968**   **1969**

The Avengers #46 (Nov. 1967) Whirlwind seeks revenge on Ant-Man and the Wasp. *(Cover by John Buscema and George Roussos)*

The Avengers #58 (Nov. 1968) The Vision joins the team. *(Cover by John Buscema and George Klein)*

The Avengers #71 (Dec. 1969) The first appearance of the Invaders. *(Cover by Sal Buscema and Sam Grainger)*

The HULK

DR. ROBERT BRUCE BANNER was a frail scientist who worked in a top-secret government research facility. While testing a new weapon, he spotted a teenager named Rick Jones on site. Banner saved Rick's life, but was exposed to massive amounts of gamma radiation, which affected his entire cellular structure. Banner now transforms into a nasty-tempered, monstrous creature called the Hulk. The Hulk may be the strongest being on Earth and his strength grows in proportion to his anger.

TEMPORARY AVENGER

The Hulk was instrumental in the formation of the Avengers. He became one of the team's founding members because he claimed he would rather join the other heroes than fight them. He changed his mind a few weeks later when the Space Phantom briefly took his identity and he found out how much the other Avengers disliked and distrusted him. He quit the team immediately and stormed off.

Friend and Foe

The Hulk possesses the intelligence of Dr. Banner on some occasions and is a mindless monster on others, so his relationship with the Avengers is a stormy one. He aided them against the alien creature Psyklop, last survivor of an insectoid race, and he joined the Avengers when Ares, god of war, conquered Olympus and attempted to invade Earth.

The Hulk weighs around 1000 lbs. (454 kg.)

Avenging Allies

The Hulk and the Sub-Mariner both hated the Avengers. They formed an alliance and ambushed the team in caves beneath the island of Gibraltar.

UNSTOPPABLE

The Hulk never tires. The longer a battle lasts, the stronger he becomes.

"THE HUMANS ARE MY SWORN ENEMIES! BECAUSE OF THEM I HAVE LOST MY BIRTH-RIGHT, MY PEOPLE, EVERYTHING I HOLD DEAR!"

"I DON'T GO FOR ALL THAT FLOWERY TALK, BUT I HATE HUMANS, TOO!"

The SUB-MARINER

PRINCE NAMOR, the son of a blue-skinned Atlantean princess and an American sea captain, was raised in the underwater kingdom of Atlantis and grew up distrusting surface dwellers. During World War II, Namor sided with the Allies against the Axis Powers, fighting alongside Captain America in the Invaders team. Some time after the war, Namor lost his memory and lived as a derelict in New York City until his memory was restored by the Human Torch. After learning that Atlantis had been destroyed, Namor turned against the human race.

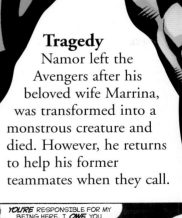

MUTANT MERMAN
The Sub-Mariner can breathe in air or under water. He has superhuman strength and wings above his heels that allow him to fly.

FROM ENEMY TO ALLY

The Sub-Mariner attacked the Avengers with the help of the Hulk, the strongest creature on land. He then forced a stranded alien to turn the heroes to stone! However, these incidents were forgotten when the original members left the

STILL THINK YOU'RE STRONGER THAN ME, LITTLE MAN??

MY POWER IS LEAVING ME, BECAUSE I HAVE BEEN OUT OF THE WATER FOR SO LONG!

I NEED THE HULK! WHERE IS HE?? HAS HE DESERTED ME?

HOLD HIM THUS, GIANT-MAN, WHILE I FIND THE HULK AGAIN! VICTORY IS NOW WITHIN OUR GRASP!

Avengers, Namor was offered a spot on the team, but refused because he was busy ruling the recently rebuilt Atlantis. The Avengers later aided him against his archenemy Attuma, who longed to usurp his throne.

Namor means "avenging son" in Atlantean.

ONE OF THE ESKIMOS TOLD THE STORY OF PERSONNEL AT A U.S. WEATHER STATION... I GOT ALL THE DETAILS A FEW MONTHS LATER. THAT'S HOW I KNOW YOU HURLED THEIR ICE-COVERED TOTEM OUT TO SEA.

Undersea Avenger
Namor eventually learned that he was actually responsible for the return of Captain America. After stumbling upon a tribe of Eskimos who were worshiping a figure frozen in ice, Namor hurled it into the sea. The ice melted to reveal Captain America. Remembering their days on the Invaders team, the grateful Cap invited Namor to join the Avengers.

Tragedy
Namor left the Avengers after his beloved wife Marrina, was transformed into a monstrous creature and died. However, he returns to help his former teammates when they call.

"BUT THE STORY DOESN'T STOP THERE, YOU SEE, THE OBJECT IN THAT BLOCK OF ICE WAS A MAN... A MAN WHO'D ACCIDENTALLY BEEN THROWN INTO A STATE OF SUSPENDED ANIMATION!

"AS THE TOTEM DRIFTED INTO THE WARM WATERS OF THE GULF STREAM, ITS ICY SHEATH SLOWLY MELTED."

"THE BODY WAS FOUND AND RECOVERED BY A SPECIAL SUBMERSIBLE CRAFT, MANNED BY THE AVENGERS...

"...JUST MINUTES BEFORE I REVIVED."

YOU MEAN--?

YOU'RE RESPONSIBLE FOR MY BEING HERE. I OWE YOU FOR THAT.

NOW, WILL YOU LET ME PUT YOUR NAME IN NOMINATION FOR AVENGERS MEMBERSHIP?

CAPTAIN AMERICA

STEVE ROGERS was a sickly young man who grew up during the economic depression of the 1930s. When the Nazis invaded Europe, Steve tried to enlist, but was rejected on health grounds. A general overheard him express his desire to serve his country and offered him a chance to join a program called Operation: Rebirth.

SUPER-SOLDIER

Steve was injected with top-secret Super-Soldier serum and his body was bombarded with "vita-rays." The treatment transformed his weak body into the pinnacle of human perfection. Though he was supposed be the first of an army of physically enhanced agents, a Nazi spy murdered the serum's inventor and Steve thus became the Army's one and only super-soldier.

SYMBOL OF FREEDOM

After intense training in gymnastics and martial arts, Steve Rogers was given a costume patterned after his country's flag and code-named Captain America.

Bucky Barnes

Orphan James Buchanan "Bucky" Barnes was a mascot at Camp Lehigh, Virginia, where Steve Rogers was stationed. After accidentally learning Steve's secret identity, Bucky trained with Captain America and gained his own costume.

BUCKY

FATAL MOMENT

Cap could only look on helplessly as Bucky tried to defuse the bomb.

Bucky's Death

Toward the end of World War II, Cap and Bucky tried to foil Baron Zemo's scheme to steal a bomb-laden drone plane. As the plane took off, Bucky leaped aboard and was killed defusing the bomb. Captain America fell into the sea, where the Super-Soldier formula caused him to enter a state of suspended animation.

Reborn

The unconscious Captain America drifted in the ocean until he became frozen in a block of ice. Decades later he was found *(below)* and revived by the newly formed Avengers. Invited to join the team, he formed a close friendship with Rick Jones, who became his partner for a while. Cap possesses superhuman strength, speed, agility, and endurance. His shield is made of an unknown, virtually indestructible alloy and is a perfectly balanced throwing weapon.

Red Skull

While working as a bellboy, Johann Schmidt met Adolf Hitler who trained him to become a Nazi super-agent. After repeatedly battling Captain America during World War II, the Red Skull was placed in suspended animation and later revived. He now runs an unnamed subversive organization dedicated to world domination.

Costume Change

Captain America's costume is one of the most instantly recognizable of all heroes'. However, he has occasionally changed his look when the situation demanded it.

THE CAPTAIN

Temporarily fired by the U.S. government, Cap wore a black version of his costume for a few months.

Discovering Captain America

Skilled in every known form of hand-to-hand combat, Captain America is also a master of strategy. He first assumed leadership of the Avengers when the original four members decided to leave and he helped recruit the new team. Though he has occasionally left for brief periods, Cap has always been a cornerstone of the Avengers. He is also a symbol of liberty and justice.

THE EX-PATRIOT

Accused of being a traitor, Cap adopted another new costume when he was temporarily exiled from his beloved America.

IN ARMOR

When his super-soldier serum mutated and left him paralyzed, Cap had to wear an armored exoskeleton designed by Tony Stark.

The Invaders

During World War II, Cap helped form the Invaders. Along with Bucky, the original Human Torch, his partner Toro and the Sub-Mariner, Cap battled the superhuman agents of the Axis Powers. Later members included Union Jack, Spitfire, the Whizzer and Miss America.

IT IS DONE! PHASE ONE IS COMPLETE! NOW TO FIND *THE AVENGERS* AND BEGIN PHASE TWO!

FOR THEY WILL BE THE REAL TEST! IF I CAN DESTROY *THE AVENGERS* SINGLE-HANDED, THEN NO POWER ON EARTH CAN STOP THE TOTAL INVASION BY MY PEOPLE!

SPACE PHANTOM

*T*HE ADVANCE SCOUT of an alien invasion force from the planet Phantus, the Space Phantom arrived on Earth shortly after the Avengers became a team. The alien quickly realized that he had to eliminate these powerful heroes in order to complete his mission. Like the rest of his highly evolved race, the Space Phantom could instantly assume the physical appearance and powers of any mortal. Whenever he duplicated someone, the original was immediately shunted into Limbo, where he or she remained until the Phantom took on another likeness or returned to his own appearance.

BUT, THE *OTHERS* APPROACH!

I MUST ACT QUICKLY! I SHALL NOW TAKE *IRON MAN'S* FORM! NEITHER THE HULK NOR GIANT-MAN WILL SUSPECT... TILL IT IS *TOO LATE*

Lost in Limbo
The Space Phantom began his attack on the Avengers by impersonating the Hulk and starting a fight with the rest of the team. But when the Phantom tried to take on Thor's identity, he discovered that his power did not work on immortal Asgardians and found himself in Limbo. After escaping, he joined the Grim Reaper and later became the pawn of Immortus, the lord of Limbo.

The LAVA MEN

*D*EEP BENEATH the Earth's surface is a network of underground caves called Subterranea, where lives a race of rock-like Lava Men. They possess skin the color of molten lava and can generate intense blasts of heat. They can also expel blasts of volcanic ash and instantly melt metal or turn it into ash. Dissatisfied with their underground existence, the Lava Men often try to invade the surface world, but are always thwarted by the Avengers.

THESE POOR FRIGHTENED CREATURES WERE THE CAUSE OF ALL THIS DAMAGE?

ALL RIGHT! WHAT'S GOING ON THERE? YOU... GET UP ON YOUR FEET AND TELL ME!

YOU ARE THE LADY-OF-LIGHT... OUR LEGENDS FORETOLD OF YOUR COMING.

I SEE. WELL, I'M HERE NOW--AND I WANT TO KNOW WHY YOU WERE DESTROYING THIS PLACE

WE DID BUT STRIKE BACK, RADIANT ONE!

TOO LONG HAVE WE DWELLED BELOW, WHILE YOU PUNY HUMANS ENJOYED THE FRUITS OF THE SURFACE!

YOUR WEAPONS ARE DISTASTEFUL TO ME! I SHALL *DESTROY* THEM - - SO!

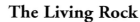

The Living Rock
The Lava Men forced a gigantic "living rock" to the surface, where it caused wholesale destruction by emitting piercing sounds. The Avengers arrived and tricked the Hulk into striking the one spot that destroyed the rock. The Lava Men also attempted to make all the volcanoes on Earth erupt, and later clashed with the Avengers again when a government agency sank a magma tap into the Earth.

LADY-OF-LIGHT
Mistaken by the Lava Men for a sacred figure from their legends, Captain Marvel stopped the battle and arranged a truce.

MINOTAUR

*T*HE LEGENDARY MINOTAUR is one of the great beasts of the Earth and is virtually immortal. Half-man and half-bull, it possesses super-strength and is incapable of feeling physical pain. Its hide is also indestructible. The monster wandered the underground world known as Subterranea for centuries until it found its way to Monster Isle, home of the hate-filled Mole Man. Determined to destroy the Avengers, the Mole Man lured them into a trap and forced them to fight the deadly Minotaur.

After Thor, Giant Man, and Iron Man leave the team, the new Avengers realized that they needed the Hulk's power. Their search led them into a confrontation with the Minotaur.

CLANG! CLANG! CLANG!

MY SHIELD HAD **NO EFFECT!** HE DIDN'T EVEN FEEL IT!

Unbeat-a-bull!
Captain America's shield proved useless against the Minotaur's tough hide and so did Hawkeye's arrows. Only by working together could the new team defeat the creature.

MOLE MAN

*B*EAUTY MAY ONLY BE skin deep, but ugliness can scar forever... the Mole Man knew no one liked him. Women ignored him and his co-workers made fun of him. Disgusted with this treatment, he journeyed to the Bermuda Triangle, entered Subterranea, and became the leader of a race of Subterraneans. He also learned to control the giant creatures living in the caverns beneath Monster Isle.

ONCE I PULL THIS SWITCH, MY NEWLY COMPLETED **ATOMIC GYROSCOPE** WILL INCREASE THE SPEED OF THE EARTH'S ROTATION ON ITS AXIS! FASTER AND FASTER THIS PLANET WILL SPIN, UNTIL...

ARMAGEDDON!
Determined to punish humanity, the Mole Man's atomic gyroscope was designed to set off massive earthquakes around the world.

Weapon of Mass Destruction
Warned by an ant colony, Giant Man realized that the Mole Man was behind a series of tremors that threatened various locales around the globe. The Avengers responded, only to learn that the Mole Man had allied himself with the Red Ghost, who could become intangible at will. The two villains threatened to destroy all life on Earth—until Giant Man shrank to ant size and sabotaged their doomsday machine.

NOW LISTEN, ALL OF YOU! THE ANTS HAVE NEVER SENT A FALSE ALARM YET! WHO KNOWS **WHAT** DANGERS THEY MAY HAVE UNEARTHED?? REMEMBER THE CASE OF THE *F.F.* AND THE *MOLE MAN* SOME MONTHS AGO?

More Mole Mayhem
After sending the Minotaur against the Avengers, the Mole Man fought for control of Subterranea. He also tried to sink California and raise a new continent. He was briefly imprisoned by the Lava Men and later asked the Avengers to help save his kingdom.

BARON ZEMO

BARON HEINRICH ZEMO was a Nazi scientist during World War II. A designer of super-weapons, he built an early laser, a "death ray" that could disintegrate almost anything. Targeted by the Allies, Zemo began to wear a red hood to conceal his identity. He was working on "Adhesive X" when Captain America broke into his lab. Cap's shield shattered the vat of adhesive and Zemo's mask was permanently glued to his head.

REVENGE

Furious with Captain America, Zemo created powerful androids that attacked British and American forces. As World War II was drawing to a close, Zemo went to London to steal an experimental drone plane. Captain America learned of his plan and arrived with his teenage partner Bucky. During their battle, Bucky was killed and Captain America was flung into the ocean, falling into a state of suspended animation.

ADHESIVE X

Zemo invented an adhesive that was so powerful it could never be dissolved. It had tremendous military potential because it could be dropped on enemy armies and glue them to the ground.

Zemo's mask had no openings, but allowed him to see and breathe.

LORD ZEMO

After the war, Zemo fled to the jungles of South America, Zemo conquered a small kingdom. The natives thought him a god and obeyed his will.

The Birth of Wonder Man

Learning that Captain America had been revived, Zemo came out of hiding and tried to kill his old foe. Zemo formed the Masters of Evil and tried to capture the Avengers with his "Adhesive X" spray. When that failed, he teamed up with the Enchantress and the Executioner. Zemo later transformed Simon Williams into the super-strong Wonder Man *(right)* and tried to use him to destroy the Avengers, but Williams chose death before dishonor.

Masters of Evil

The Masters of Evil were formed by the first Baron Zemo. The team consisted of the Melter, who possessed a device that could melt solid objects and often fought Iron Man, the Radioactive Man, a living nuclear reactor who battled Thor and the Black Knight, an armored warrior who frequently challenged Giant-Man. The Executioner and the Enchantress later joined the team, which disbanded shortly after Baron Zemo's death.

...YOUR END WILL BE MY TRIUMPH..!

NOT TODAY!

Crushed to Death
Zemo kidnapped Rick Jones and brought him to South America. When the Avengers tried to rescue the teenager, they were ambushed by the Masters of Evil and Captain America had to go to Zemo's base alone. When Captain America finally confronted the man who had murdered his friend Bucky, his shield temporarily blinded Zemo who accidentally caused a landslide that crushed him.

UFFN--!

SON OF ZEMO
Helmut Zemo swore to get revenge on Captain America for killing his father. Wearing a similar costume, the new Baron Zemo tried to drown Cap and the Falcon in a boiling vat of "Adhesive X."

HERE'S A COUPLE PRIZES FOR YOU, BARON!

AIN'T THAT SWORD S'POSED TO BE INDESTRUCTIBLE?

YES, WRECKER, THERE'S EVEN RUMORED TO BE A SORT OF... ENCHANTMENT ABOUT IT.

A Bitter Enemy
During the battle, the searing liquid splashed Helmut and his face was horribly scarred. Zemo later sent an army of mutates after Cap and formed a brief alliance with the Red Skull. He later organized a new Masters of Evil and invaded Avengers Mansion. When the Avengers temporarily disappeared from this reality, Zemo gathered his Masters of Evil and refit them with new, "heroic" identities as the Thunderbolts.

Helmut took the identity of Citizen V, a British costumed hero murdered by the first Zemo.

HAVE WE GOT A TALE FOR YOU!! PLEASE DON'T FRUSTRATE US. YOU'VE GOT TO READ IT!!

Introducing ZEMO! and his MASTERS OF EVIL!

A later version of the Masters included the Melter, Radioactive Man, Klaw, master of sound, and Whirlwind, who could spin at superhuman speed.

The latest team: Titania, Absorbing Man, Moonstone, Yellowjacket, Grey Gargoyle, the Fixer, Tiger Shark, Goliath, Blackout, Whirlwind, and Mr. Hyde.

ENCHANTRESS

Amora uses magic to enhance her beauty and to enslave any man who kisses her.

AMORA THE ENCHANTRESS was born in Asgard, home of the Norse Gods. She studied magic under the guidance of Karnilla, Queen of the Norns, but was dismissed for being too undisciplined. Undaunted, the Enchantress used her youth and beauty to persuade many of Asgard's greatest wizards to share their secrets with her. She soon became a sorceress of great knowledge and power.

> HOW YOU MUST *HATE* THE MIGHTY THUNDER GOD, LOKI! I KNOW 'TWAS *YOU* WHO GAVE THIS PLAN TO ODIN! BUT NO MATTER...I SHALL CARRY OUT THIS MISSION...FOR LONG HAVE I WISHED TO CONQUER THE HEART OF HANDSOME THOR!

SECRET PASSION
Loki once asked Amora to make Thor her slave. She agreed because she was secretly in love with the thunder god.

> I AM YOUR MASTER! YOU MUST OBEY THE ENCHANTRESS!!

MISTRESS OF MISCHIEF

Exiled from Asgard because of her evil deeds, the Enchantress and her partner the Executioner joined with Baron Zemo. She used magic to make Thor attack his fellow Avengers. He battled Giant-Man and the Wasp before Iron Man woke him from his trance. The Enchantress also helped Zemo create Wonder Man and her sorcery saved the Masters of Evil from Immortus.

Stirring Up Trouble
Amora hated the Avengers so much that she used one of Zemo's machines to create the villain Power Man. After failing to conquer Asgard herself, Amora was Loki's chief lieutenant when he briefly became ruler. Pretending to repent of her past crimes, Amora even become Thor's girlfriend for a while, but she soon returned to her wicked ways.

While posing as the Valkyrie, Amora once convinced all the female Avengers to attack the male members.

> FROM NOW ON, IT'S THE *VALKYRIE* AND HER LADY *LIBERATORS!*

Like all Asgardians, Amora is virtually immortal and possesses superhuman strength and endurance.

32

EXECUTIONER

THE SON OF A FROST GIANT and an Asgardian goddess, Skurge chose the life of a warrior. He became known as the Executioner when he helped the Norse Gods win a war against the Storm Giants. Skurge fell in love with Amora the Enchantress as soon as he laid eyes on her. He desperately tried to win her heart, but she treated him more like a pet than a lover.

THE EXECUTIONER'S SAD SONG

Exiled to Earth for attempting to kill Thor, Skurge became one of Baron Zemo's Masters of Evil; his hatred for Thor often led him to attack the Avengers. Skurge also aided Loki on many occasions. Once, fed up with Amora's disdainful treatment, he left her and journeyed into the future in a bid to establish an empire. He later returned to Amora and they invaded Asgard together with a troll army—only to be defeated by Thor.

ENCHANTRESS! YOU HAVE COME TO ME AT LAST! DOES THIS MEAN YOU WILL BE MINE??

NOT YET, MY POWERFUL FRIEND! BUT PERHAPS, IF YOU ACCOMPLISH A SIMPLE TASK FOR ME, I SHALL LOOK UPON YOU WITH GREATER FAVOR!

ANYTHING, BEAUTIFUL ONE! I AM YOURS TO COMMAND! I WOULD BATTLE ALL OF ASGARD TO WIN YOUR HEART!

THAT WILL NOT BE NECESSARY! I WANT YOU TO GO TO EARTH...

GREEN-EYED MONSTERS
When she learned that Thor had fallen in love with Jane Foster, Amora become jealous and sent Skurge to kidnap her. He exiled the mortal woman to another dimension and tried to humiliate the thunder god in battle.

Skurge longed to crush Thor because Amora loved him.

Skurge was a true warrior-born, a master of combat and almost as strong as Thor.

...AND BEGINS TO DO THE THING HE DOES BEST!

Redemption at Last
Despite his past crimes, Skurge teamed-up with Thor when Surtur, an enormous fiery demon, attempted to destroy Asgard. Skurge was later shocked to discover that Amora had fallen in love with someone else. Having nothing to live for, he joined Thor on a quest to the land of the dead, where he heroically sacrificed himself to save his former enemy. His spirit now resides in Valhalla, although it has occasionally ventured forth to aid Thor.

MAGIC AX
Skurge carried a double-bladed, magical ax that could rip open rifts in time and space so that he could travel between dimensions. It also fired blasts of intense cold or heat.

KANG

Kang learned that his ancestor was Nathaniel Richards, the father of Mr. Fantastic, Reed Richards.

*H*E WAS BORN to conquer. The child destined to be Kang was born in the 30th Century of one of Earth's possible futures. Although his world sparkled with peace and prosperity, he craved action and studied the great warriors of the past. He constructed a great timeship that was modeled to resemble the Sphinx. Traveling to ancient Egypt, he used his scientific knowledge and advanced weaponry to become the absolute monarch of the ancient world.

THE CONQUEROR

Calling himself Rama-Tut, Kang ruled Egypt until the Fantastic Four journeyed back in time and forced him to flee into the timestream. He overshot the 30th century and arrived in the war-torn 40th century. He soon made himself master of that time period and then decided to extend his empire to include other eras.

NEW SHIP
Kang replaced his Sphinx-like timeship with a heavily-armed craft.

REVENGE BID
Determined to get his revenge on the Fantastic Four, Kang decided to add their time period to his burgeoning empire.

THERE HE *IS!* He seems to be sitting in some sort of transparent anti-grav seat!!

NO NEED FOR SUCH UNSEEMLY SPEED! *TIME* MEANS NOTHING TO *KANG, THE CONQUEROR!!*

I FIND HIS *CONFIDENCE* DISTURBING! HE SEEMS TO HAVE NO FEAR OF OUR POWER!!

I'LL BET HE'S NOT BAD-LOOKING UNDER THAT SILLY HEAD-GEAR HE'S WEARING!

I SCOFF AT YOUR ARROW, AVENGER! YOU ARE TOO *WEAK* TO SLAY ME IN COLD BLOOD!

THUS, WHILE YOU HESITATE MY SIGNAL *DOOMS* AN EMPIRE!

THIS IS IT! THE *FOUR* OF US AGAINST KANG'S INVINCIBLE LEGIONS NOW!

A Change of Target

Kang journeyed to the present and landed his warship near Washington D.C. To his surprise, the authorities summoned the newly-formed Avengers instead of the Fantastic Four. Kang soon caught the team in a tractor beam and imprisoned them in his ship. Rick Jones and his Teen Brigade freed the Avengers, who deactivated Kang's battlesuit and forced him to flee back to the future—thereby earning his eternal enmity.

BID TOMORROW GOOD-BYE!

THE ULTIMATE PRIZE
The membership changed, but Kang didn't care. He longed to crush the Avengers and conquer the one era that eluded his grasp— the present.

A Formidable Foe

Kang is a brilliant scientist and strategist. His body armor is composed of metal alloys that are only available in the 40th century. The battlesuit grants him superhuman strength and is equipped with a 30-day supply of air and food. It contains a force-field projector powerful enough to withstand blows from Thor's hammer. Kang's gauntlets project an anti-gravitational beam and can also fire concussive blasts.

For Love of Ravonna

Kang fell in love with the beautiful Princess Ravonna, ruler of the last unconquered kingdom on an alternate future Earth. Bringing the Avengers to her time, he tried to impress her by defeating them, but she was severely injured by one of his underlings. However, nothing could diminish Kang's unrequited passion.

Immortus

Whenever Kang traveled through time, he created alternate timelines and duplicates of himself. One of these duplicates stumbled into realm beyond time. Calling himself Immortus, he renounced his past attempts at conquest and began to untangle the many timelines Kang had accidentally created. Immortus believed he knew what was best for the timestream and thus clashed with both his other selves and the Avengers.

Along Came a Spider...

Kang decided to attack the Avengers with a robot duplicate of Spider-Man. He built the automaton and sent it into the past, where it lured Giant-Man and the Wasp into a trap. When Thor appeared, the robot tricked him into changing back into Dr. Don Blake. Though the robot also managed to defeat Captain America, the real Spider-Man caught on to Kang's plan, fought the robot, and deactivated it. Kang had been foiled once more.

Scarlet Centurion

An alternate version of Rama-Tut became trapped in a time storm and ended up in the 20th century. Adopting the new identity of the Scarlet Centurion, he created a divergent timeline where he contacted the original Avengers shortly after their formation. He convinced them to take over the world for its own good and to imprison all other super beings.

THE GROWING MAN

Originally the size of a child's doll, the Growing Man can reach enormous heights by absorbing any blast, blow, or energy directed at it. Kang has used it against Thor, Iron Man, and the entire Avengers team.

WONDER MAN

SIMON WILLIAMS was a disgraced businessman who went to work for Baron Zemo. An experimental "ionic ray" treatment gave him superhuman strength, but a deadly side-effect made him reliant on regular doses of an antidote that Zemo would only provide if Simon destroyed the Avengers. In time Wonder Man rebelled, sacrificing himself to save Earth's mightiest heroes.

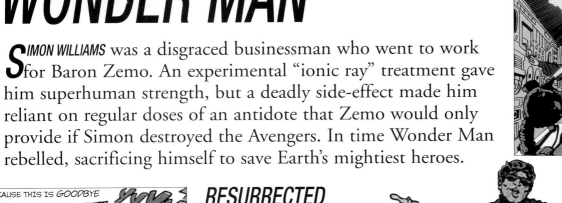

RESURRECTED

Instead of dying, Wonder Man fell into a coma-like state for many years. His body mutated until it became pure ionic energy. He eventually awoke and accused the Vision of stealing his mind. After they settled their differences, Wonder Man was invited to join the Avengers.

...'CAUSE THIS IS *GOODBYE*

IF YOU *ARE* WONDER MAN... THEN YOU *DIED* BEFORE MY TIME.

THUS, YOU CAN BE *FORGIVEN* FOR NOT KNOWING THAT I CAN MAKE MY BODY *HARD AS DIAMOND*...

IONIC RAYS
Baron Zemo's program of "ionic" radiation treatments turned Simon Williams into Wonder Man, strong as mighty Thor himself.

Mr. Hollywood
Wonder Man formed a close friendship with the Beast and they often teamed up to party or go on adventures. Wonder Man subsequently moved to Los Angeles to pursue a career in the movies and joined the West Coast Avengers.

And, as the smoke clears in the chamber below...

WE APPRECIATE YOUR HELP--BUT WHO *ARE* YOU? WHERE ARE YOU *FROM*?

I AM CALLED *WONDER-MAN*, AND I AM FROM THE HEART OF THE AMAZON JUNGLES!

Wonder Man never lost his ability to surprise the Avengers.

WONDER MAN!

UHMM-M!

Back From the Dead
A few years after he nobly gave his life to protect the Avengers from Baron Zemo's malice, Wonder Man was awakened from his coma by the Black Talon, a voodoo priest who could control zombies. Wonder Man has apparently been destroyed on many other occasions, but is virtually immortal because his ionic body always reforms itself.

The GRIM REAPER

ERIC WILLIAMS commenced his career in villainy by joining the Maggia criminal organization and convincing his younger brother Simon to embezzle a large sum of money. Simon was arrested, joined Baron Zemo, became Wonder Man, and apparently died. When Eric learned of Simon's death, he blamed the Avengers and swore vengeance as the Grim Reaper.

The Reaper's scythe has an electromagnetic blaster and a high-speed propeller blade.

Fused to the Reaper's right hand, the scythe can make victims fall into comas.

> BEHOLD, VISION-- THE LIFELESS, YET LONG-PRESERVED BODY OF ONE SIMON WILLIAMS, ONCE CALLED WONDER MAN

> AS YOU WELL KNOW, IT IS *HIS* BRAIN-PATTERNS WHICH FORMED THE BASIS OF YOUR *OWN* ARTIFICIAL MIND.

> *HE* WAS MY BROTHER --AND *SO,* LIKE IT OR NOT, ARE *YOU!*

> JOIN ME, AND I CAN TRANSFER YOUR PRESENT BRAIN *INTO* THAT BODY--- AND *MAKE IT LIVE AGAIN!*

> NO! IT-- ISN'T POSSIBLE--!

DEATH COMES CALLING

Catching Hawkeye, Goliath and the Wasp by surprise, the Reaper left them all in deep comas. He then discovered that the Vision possessed his brother's brain patterns and tried to convince the synthozoid to transfer his mind into Wonder Man's comatose body. When that failed, he hired the Black Talon to resurrect Simon as a zombie.

Trial and Tragedy

After Simon's revival, the Reaper captured the Avengers and held a trial to decide if the Vision or Wonder Man was his real brother. He decided to kill them both, but his plan failed and he was the one who died. The Reaper was later resurrected by Nekra, a vampire-like ally.

> WILLIAMS ERIC

> CHK·CHK

> WILLIAMS

> F-FREE..

> CHKK

> FREE AT LAST!

Fear the Reaper

In his current incarnation, the Grim Reaper is the personification of death. He has become a spirit, with the power to absorb human life-forces.

AND NOW, INASMUCH AS MOST *OTHER* COSTUMED ADVENTURERS CHOOSE TO WEAR MASKS, *HAWKEYE* WILL DO THE SAME!

HAWKEYE

Hawkeye has a trick arrow for every occasion.

CLINT BARTON and his older brother Barney were orphans who ran away to join a traveling carnival. At age 14, Clint attracted the attention of the show's star attraction Jacques Duquesne, the Swordsman. Duquesne began to train Clint in the art of throwing knives but, realizing the boy was a natural archer, he turned him over to Trickshot, the carnival's archer.

THE MARKSMAN

Under his new teacher, Clint mastered the bow and arrow and took the stage name Hawkeye the Marksman. While Clint trained for eight hours every day, Barney was given menial chores. Clint later learned that Duquesne had robbed the carnival's payroll to pay his gambling debts. When Clint refused to become his partner, Duquesne chased the boy onto a tightrope and then cut it from under him.

HAWKEYE'S BOWS

Hawkeye employs a number of custom-made bows for ordinary use, for distant shooting and for firing his trick arrows.

JUST THEN, AN IRONIC DEVELOPMENT OCCURS! ATTRACTED BY THE NOISE, THE *POLICE* ARRIVE, AND...

DON'T MOVE!! WE CAUGHT YOUR PARTNER, AND WE'VE GOT *YOU* DEAD TO RIGHTS!

THEY THINK I HELPED ROB THE STORE!

Mistaken Identity

After recovering from his injuries, Clint rejoined the carnival. He was inspired to become a hero by seeing Iron Man in action and tried to use his archery skills to prevent a robbery. Unfortunately, the police mistook him for a thief and he found himself battling Iron Man.

...THE DARING, DAZZLING DANGEROUS *BLACK WIDOW!!*

LADY, WHOEVER YOU ARE DON'T PINCH ME! THIS IS ONE DREAM I DON'T *EVER* WANT TO WAKE UP FROM!

I ASSURE YOU, MY COSTUMED FRIEND, THIS IS NO DREAM!

LOVE-STRUCK

Hawkeye met the Black Widow while escaping the police. He was soon committing crimes to impress her.

Sky bike

Hawkeye travels through the air on a custom-built vehicle that is modeled after a commercial snowmobile. Powered by high-speed turbines, Hawkeye's Sky-Cycle can carry up to 450 lbs (204 kg.) and travel at 380 mph (611.5 km/h. It can soar to a height of nearly 12,000 ft (3,658 meters).

> I WAS *RIGHT!!* IT'S-- HAWKEYE!!
> LOOK! TONY STARK'S BUTLER IS TIED UP-- *THAT'S* HOW HE MANAGED TO GET IN!
> STOP--ALL OF YOU!

THUNDERBOLTS

Because of his own checkered past, Hawkeye was sympathetic to the Thunderbolts, a team of former super-villains who became heroes, and even led them for a while.

The Old Order Changeth

When the Black Widow decided to quit being a spy, she was wounded by assassins. The attack made Hawkeye reassess his life: he wanted to fight criminals, not be one. He begged to be admitted into the Avengers. Impressed by his sincerity, his old enemy Iron Man sponsored him for membership. Hawkeye joined Captain America, Quicksilver and the Scarlet Witch when Thor, Iron Man, Giant-Man, and the Wasp left the team. But the transition wasn't easy for the world's greatest archer.

> EXACTLY ONE HOUR LATER, AFTER CAP'S BRIEFING...
> ARE THERE ANY QUESTIONS?
> COME *OFF* IT, GLAMOR PANTS! WE'RE NOT KIDS! WE GET THE MESSAGE!
> HOLD YOUR TONGUE HAWKEYE! *WE* DO NOT "GET THE MESSAGE"!

> YOU'RE WARNING *ME?!!* YOU OVERRATED HAS-BEEN, I'VE BEEN *ITCHIN'* FOR A CHANCE TO CHANGE THAT PARTING IN YOUR HAIR!
> OKAY, HAWKEYE! I GUESS IT'S TIME I TAUGHT YOU THAT YOUR JUNIOR ROBIN HOOD KIT DOESN'T GIVE YOU THE RIGHT TO THROW YOUR WEIGHT AROUND!

> --SO TO KEEP THE GROUP FROM BE-COMING A MOB, HE AUTHORIZED YOURS TRULY TO SET UP A CALIFORNIA EXPANSION TEAM! AND THAT'S US...
> ...THE WEST COAST AVENGERS!

GO WEST!

Hawkeye was assigned to set up a West Coast branch of the Avengers, based in California.

Part of a Team

Young and egotistical, Hawkeye wasn't used to taking orders and often argued with Captain America. However, the archer slowly gained respect for his leader and learned the value of teamwork. Believing that he wasn't contributing enough to the team, Hawkeye borrowed Hank Pym's growth formula for a while and became a new Goliath. During this time, he captured the criminal genius Egghead who was responsible for the death of his brother Barney. After returning to his bow, Hawkeye temporarily joined the Defenders and fought on their side when they battled the Avengers.

Wedded Warriors

While on temporary leave from the Avengers, Hawkeye met and married Mockingbird, who joined him on the West Coast Avengers. Their marriage had its ups and downs, but they were together when she was killed in combat.

Mockingbird

Biologist Barbara "Bobbi" Morse joined a government project to rediscover the Super-Soldier formula that transformed Steve Rogers into Captain America. She later became a S.H.I.E.L.D. agent. After a number of missions, she resigned and took on a costumed identity, calling herself first "the Huntress" and later "Mockingbird." While investigating a corrupt corporation, she met Hawkeye, her future husband. She joined him on the West Coast Avengers team, but they become estranged when she allowed an enemy to fall to his death. Mockingbird started her own short-lived team with Moon Knight and Tigra and helped train the Great Lakes Avengers. She and Hawkeye were reconciled by the time of her sad death, during a battle with the demon Mephisto.

ACE OF CLUBS

Mockingbird's battle-staves could be extended into bo sticks, javelins, or a vaulter's pole.

SACRED DEBT

Believing that they owed their lives to Magneto, the Scarlet Witch and Quicksilver joined his Brotherhood of Evil Mutants.

SCARLET WITCH

Raised in the Eastern European country of Transia by a gypsy couple, Wanda Maximoff soon learned that she had the uncanny ability to cast hexes that caused very strange things to happen. When she accidentally caused a house to burst into flame, the startled villagers almost stoned her to death as a witch. Wanda and her twin brother Pietro were saved by Magneto, the master of magnetism, who realized that the two teenagers were mutants with potentially incredible powers.

MUTANT AVENGERS

Unaware that Magneto was their real father, Wanda and Pietro took on costumed identities, as the Scarlet Witch and Quicksilver respectively, and aided him in his war against humanity. After many battles with the X-Men, the twins abandoned Magneto and were offered a chance to join the Avengers in return for full pardons for their past crimes. Pietro eventually left the team, but Wanda decided to stay. She became attracted to the Vision and began a long romance with him.

CHAOS MAGIC

The Scarlet Witch can affect probability and cause unlikely events to happen.

UNHAPPY MARRIAGE

Despite her brother Pietro's objections, Wanda married the Vision. They left the Avengers, set up house in New Jersey, and were very happy—until the Vision lost his human emotions. The couple were soon divorced.

Spells of Madness

Wanda began to study real magic and to combine it with her natural mutant abilities. However she paid a terrible price for her increased powers: she began to lose her grip on reality, conjuring up imaginary children and repeatedly experiencing bouts of insanity, during which she attacked the Avengers.

DISASSEMBLED

During one breakdown, Wanda launched an attack that resulted in the destruction of the Avengers' mansion and a number of deaths. She then tried to make the world fit her mad take on reality.

QUICKSILVER

THE WORLD HAS ALWAYS moved too slowly for Pietro Maximoff. Born with superhuman speed and reflexes, he is the son of Magneto, the world's most dangerous mutant super-criminal. Pietro's mother fled to Eastern Europe, desperate to protect her children from their father's evil influence. She gave Pietro and his twin sister Wanda up for adoption and the children became inseparable.

Quicksilver is fast enough to create a cyclone by running in a circle at super-speed.

REBELLIOUS NATURE

When he first joined the Avengers, Quicksilver often questioned Captain America's authority, but eventually grew to respect him.

QUICK DECISIONS

When Magneto saved Wanda from being stoned as a witch, Pietro reluctantly joined his Brotherhood of Evil Mutants with her. Although he distrusted humanity because of its suspicion of mutants, Pietro left the Brotherhood to join the Avengers.

Rapid Responses

Pietro left the Avengers to live with his new wife, Crystal of the Inhumans. After the birth of their daughter, they quarreled and Pietro vented his anger by attacking the Avengers. He redeemed himself by helping to rescue the Scarlet Witch, who had been brainwashed by Magneto. He then joined X-Factor, a government team of mutants.

THE WORLD'S FASTEST

Quicksilver is impatient and easily annoyed because, as far as he is concerned, everyone else always seems to be moving and thinking in slow motion! His entire body is geared toward high-speed running and he can reach speeds of 175 mph (400 km/h).

BLACK WIDOW

WAIT, NATASHA! NO MATTER WHO HE IS...OR WHAT HE'S *DONE*--YOU *CAN'T* KILL HIM!

I HAVE NO *CHOICE*, MY DARLING...

IF WE ARE ALL TO DIE, THEN I SHALL MAKE CERTAIN THAT *IXAR* DOES NOT LIVE TO BOAST OF HIS *VICTORY*!

NATALIA ALIANOVNA ROMANOVA is an orphan who was found and raised by a Russian soldier, who would one day become her chauffeur. In her teens, Natasha, as friends called her, proved to be a brilliant scholar and a gifted athlete and ballet dancer. She later married a renowned Soviet test pilot. After her husband was reported killed, Natasha honored his memory by joining the KGB and training as a spy.

MEANWHILE, IN A LUXURIOUS SUBURB, JUST OUTSIDE THE CITY, TWO OTHERS EVINCE A GREAT INTEREST IN THE AFFAIRS OF IRON MAN!

WE WILL BRING ADDITIONAL BULLETINS ABOUT ANTHONY STARK'S DISAPPEARANCE AS THEY OCCUR! NOW WE RETURN TO...

DID YOU *HEAR* THAT, HAWKEYE? THE ACCURSED *IRON MAN* IS UNDER SUSPICION IN STARK'S DISAPPEARANCE!

I HEARD, NATASHA!

STRONG AS HE IS, HE IS *PUTTY* IN THE HANDS OF THE BLACK WIDOW!

VERY WELL, MY DARLING... I'LL *DO* IT!

HAWKEYE HOOKED
The Black Widow couldn't allow herself to return Hawkeye's love.

THE SECRET AGENT

The Black Widow never trained to be a costumed agent. She was only supposed to be a spy. Her first major mission was to help assassinate an employee of Stark Industries, but Iron Man stopped her. She soon met Hawkeye, who quickly fell in love with her. On the run from the police, Hawkeye willingly teamed-up with her against Iron Man. However, Natasha gradually grew disillusioned with her Soviet masters. She decided to defect to the West, but was seriously wounded.

The Widow is a master of many martial arts.

USE *CAUTION*, COLONEL FURY! SHE'S LISTED ON OUR FILES AS *EXTREMELY DANGEROUS*!

YOU CALLED HIM-- *COLONEL FURY*?

Agent of S.H.I.E.L.D
After a brief reunion with Hawkeye, the Widow offered her services to Nick Fury and S.H.I.E.L.D. She performed numerous missions for this worldwide intelligence and peacekeeping organization.

Called to Assemble
After helping the Avengers battle Magneto and the Lion-God, the Black Widow led a super-team called the Champions, who helped the Avengers rescue Hercules from the giant immortal Typhon. After the Champions disbanded, the Widow was invited to join the Avengers. On her first mission, she faced the Tetrarchs of Entropy, powerful alien caretakers of a dimension full of exiles and super-prisoners.

THIS *CHAIN BELT* I'VE ADDED WILL BE *MORE* THAN DECORATIVE!

IT'LL HOLD MY SPARE *WEB-LINE*... AND STORE THE *POWERLETS* FOR MY *WIDOW'S BITE*!

WIDOW'S BITE
The Widow carries various grenades, a cable line, and a wrist-blaster she calls her "Widow's Bite."

FOOLS! DID YOU THINK TO CAPTURE ONE WHO CAN RACE ALONG THE SHEEREST *WALLS*?

THEY ARE *CRACK SHOTS*! I AM FORTUNATE THAT MY FLEXIBLE *SUCTION SHOES* ALLOW ME TO ELUDE THEM!

NOW TO ROUND THIS BUILDING-- AND FADE INTO THE *DARKNESS*!

SWORDSMAN

JACQUES DUQUESNE grew up admiring a relative known as the Crimson Cavalier, a costumed hero who fought against the Nazis. When he heard that the country of Sin-Cong was fighting for independence, Jacques became the Swordsman and joined the revolutionaries. He later renounced political activism and chose to become a mercenary.

NOW IS THE HOUR!

...TO BECOME A LIVING SYMBOL OF HOPE... FREEDOM...

NOW I CAN UNDER-STAND WHY MEN SUCH AS THE CAVALIER, OR CAPTAIN AMERICA TOOK SUCH A ROLE...

...AND JUSTICE! JUSTICE LONG-DEFERRED!

The Swordsman is a master of throwing knives and other bladed weapons, and skilled in unarmed combat.

UNREPENTANT

DID YOU HEAR ABOUT THE PAYMASTER BEING ROBBED, AND--WHA'--?? WHERE'D YOU GET ALL THAT MONEY??

YOU LITTLE PUNK! I WARNED YA NEVER TO COME IN HERE WITHOUT ASKING FIRST!!

Jacques performed in a circus, befriending young Clint Barton. When Jacques robbed the circus payroll Clint turned against him, and the Swordsman fled to Europe becoming a notorious criminal. He then offered his services to the Avengers, hoping to use them to commit even greater crimes.

A Hero's Death

The Avengers turned down the Swordsman, who joined the Mandarin and attempted to destroy them. However, he grew to admire the team—especially the Scarlet Witch and Mantis, with whom he fell in love. She refused to date a criminal so he turned his life around. Now a champion for justice, the Swordsman begged the Avengers for a second chance. He proved himself a valuable ally, but Mantis still kept her distance. Battling the tyrant Kang, the Swordsman gave his life to save her.

AND THEN, ONE DAY-- DURING A REST PERIOD--

THEY'RE NOT LOOKING! THIS IS MY CHANCE TO COMPLETE THE MANDARIN'S TRAP--!

I'M JUST...ONE OF THOSE PEOPLE...

...WHO DOESN'T...

...COUNT.

DARLING!

SACRIFICE
Mortally wounded by Kang, the Swordsman died in the arms of grief-stricken Mantis.

THIS IS THE END OF LIFE AS YOU HAVE KNOWN IT, BELOVED. HAVE YOU ANY REGRETS.. DOUBTS?

NONE, BELOVED. THIS ONE HAS LIVED AS SHE WOULD--AND NOW, WE TWO SHALL LIVE AS WE WILL!

The Second Swordsman

A few years later, the Avengers met a new Swordsman, from an alternate Earth that had been destroyed. His life story, skills and personality are identical to the original. The new Swordsman travels the world with Magdalene (see p.112). They aid the Avengers whenever called.

SUPER SWORD

By pressing various buttons on his sword, the Swordsman can project blasts of electrical energy, disintegration rays and streams of flame or nerve gas.

IT IS MY *FATHER...* THE VENERATED *ZEUS!!* HAIL, SUPREME ONE.

ZEUS! THE MONARCH OF OLYMPUS, EVEN AS *ODIN* IS LORD OF ASGARD!

I HAVE WITNESSED YOUR BATTLE AND FOUND IT HONORABLE! IN TRUTH, YOU ARE *EACH* DESERVING OF *VICTORY!*

HERCULES

BORN NEARLY three thousand years ago, Hercules is the son of Zeus, king of the gods of Olympus, and a mortal woman. As a baby, he exhibited his extraordinary strength by strangling two serpents that attacked him. His strength grew until he became the most powerful Olympian of all. In Greek myth, Hercules is best known for his Twelve Labors, which he carried out to prove himself worthy of immortality.

The golden mace of Hercules is virtually indestructible and has survived direct blows from Thor's hammer.

Hercules is an expert at all forms of hand-to-hand combat.

MY BROTHER, MY ENEMY

Ares, the Olympian God of War, has frequently attempted to overthrow Zeus and conquer Olympus; however, Hercules, his half-brother, always ruins his plans. Ares is a true warrior born. He is nearly as strong as Hercules and is highly skilled with various ancient weapons.

AND NOW, WE MUST MOMENTARILY AVERT OUR EYES FROM THE SILENT PLIGHT OF THE LOVELY *NATASHA* -- AND TURN THEM TOWARDS THE TOWERING PEAK OF A TIMELESS *MOUNTAIN,* WHERE ARE HEARD THE CLAMOROUS *SOUNDS* OF TURBULENT *COMBAT--!*

HAVE AT THEE, *GOD OF WAR!* FOR YOU, HERCULES, THE MATCHLESS *MACE* OF *HERCULES* SHALL SOON MAKE THEE CRY-- *HOLD,* ENOW!

THWANG!

The Gift

Known throughout Olympus as the Prince of Power, Hercules relishes the thrills and joys of battle. He also believes that it is a great honor to fight him and often bestows this so-called "gift" on both friends and foes alike. Instead of a handshake, Hercules often greets his fellow Avengers with a friendly punch in the face.

--IT'S TIME FOR YOU TO--

--DIE!!

SPWA-KWOOM

HOME AWAY FROM HOME

Hercules returns to Earth and rejoins the Avengers whenever his father exiles him from Olympus for being disobedient.

"REMEMBER MY LOVE FOR YOU, HERCULES. ABOVE ALL ELSE, REMEMBER THAT."

TAYLOR

Lovelorn Hero

With the aid of Ares, Hercules' stepmother Hera played a nasty trick on Hercules. She conjured up an illusion of a woman and cast a spell to make Hercules fall in love with it. He was heartbroken when he learned the truth.

HE GAVE HIS NAME AS *POWERS* -- AND I BELIEVE IT!

WHAT A *GROOVY* HUNK OF *MALE!*

THOUGH THY WORDS BE STRANGE, DAMSELS, THY TONE IS ONE OF *FRIENDSHIP!*

COULDST THOU TELL ME IF SOME EARTHLY *SUSTENANCE* MAY BE OBTAINED HEREIN?

IS HE FOR *REAL?*

POWER MAN

ERIK JOSTEN was a smuggler and soldier of fortune who worked for Baron Zemo. After he was killed, Erik searched Zemo's old hideout and found the machine that had given Wonder Man superhuman powers. With the Enchantress' help, Erik activated the machine. He became as strong as mighty Thor and called himself Power Man.

ZEMO'S LABORATORY
Erik Josten had no idea how to work Zemo's machines. However, the Enchantress had no such problems. She saw the chance of creating a new super-being to challenge the Avengers.

THIS POWER FOR HIRE

In love with the Enchantress, Erik tried to help her destroy the Avengers. Using a series of illusions, she managed to turn New York City against the heroes, but later deserted Erik and fled when the Avengers regrouped and teamed up against her. Erik joined with the Swordsman and fought the Avengers for various employers, such as the Mandarin, the Red Skull and Count Nefaria.

Awesome Attack
Power Man, the Swordsman, and Black Widow made a formidable team, but the malevolent trio were caught unawares in their hideout by a blistering attack by Henry Pym in Goliath mode.

BAD GOLIATH
Erik gained the ability to increase his size and changed his name to Goliath. He can grow to a height of 60 ft (18.3 meters); he gains in strength as his size increases.

Power Man received extensive combat training while a mercenary.

The COLLECTOR

OF COURSE! FORGIVE ME FOR NOT INTRODUCING MYSELF! I AM--THE COLLECTOR!

I HAVE SPENT A *LIFETIME* SECRETLY COLLECTING THE GREATEST PRIZES OF ALL! IN FACT I SEE ONE OF MY MOST *RECENT* ACQUISITIONS APPROACHING ME *NOW*--!

TANELEER TIVAN is one of the oldest creatures in the universe. Virtually immortal, he lived a tranquil existence with his wife and daughter for centuries beyond number. After his daughter reached maturity and left them, his wife lost the will to live and ceased to exist. Taneleer decided that he needed a hobby: he began collecting living beings and artifacts of great power.

IN THE COLLECTOR'S CLUTCHES

As eons passed, Taneleer's obsession with collecting grew. He became interested in the Avengers and schemed to add the Wasp to his collection, but Goliath saved her. He later used a potion to gain control of Thor and sent him to capture Iron Man, but the other Avengers drove him away.

THEN, WITH THE MEREST TURNING OF A DIAL...

IRON MAN!

AT THIS VERY *MOMENT*, HE RETURNS TO THE CITY FROM SOME *PERILOUS* ADVENTURE!

BUT, WHATEVER IT MAY HAVE BEEN... IT CANNOT COMPARE WITH THAT WHICH *AWAITS* HIM!

THEN, WHEN THE VALIANT QUINTET HAS RECOVERED CONSCIOUSNESS...

YOU ARE ALL THE SAME SIZE! WHERE IS *GIANT-MAN*?? I MUST *HAVE* HIM -- TO COMPLETE MY COLLECTION!

I NEED BOTH THE WASP *AND* GIANT MAN TO HAVE A *FULL SET!*

The Clash with Korvac

The Collector sent his daughter, Carina Walters, to spy on a near-omnipotent individual named Michael Korvac. Unfortunately she fell in love with Korvac, who slew her father. The Collector's kinsman, the Grandmaster, later challenged Death to a contest, hoping to resurrect the Collector. He was finally revived and has returned to his hobby: collecting.

POSSIBLE FUTURES

The Collector is one of the Elders of the Universe and possesses the ability to see into the future. However, his visions only show him what can happen, not necessarily what will actually occur.

I'VE *DONE* IT! I'VE MANAGED TO PUT *EACH* OF THEM UNDER THE RAYS OF THE *TIME TRANSCENDER* BEAMS!

FOR THEM, TIME WILL APPEAR TO BE *STANDING STILL*, UNTIL THE LIGHTS ARE AGAIN SHUT OFF!

AND NOW FOR THE *FINAL* PART OF MY *INFALLIBLE* PLAN!

COUNT NEFARIA

Count Nefaria is virtually immortal because his ionic body always seems to find a way to reform itself.

COUNT *LUCHINO NEFARIA* was the descendant of a long line of Italian noblemen. He was also a member of the Maggia crime syndicate. When the Avengers captured several key Maggia players, Nefaria inveigled the team to his castle and held them in suspended animation. While they were asleep, he projected holograms of the Avengers that threatened to seize control of the U.S.

LIVING NIGHTMARES

The Avengers eventually awoke and cleared their names. Nefaria later returned with a machine that could project highly realistic nightmares. He planned to use this machine to kill the Avengers and began with Iron Man, pitting him against many of his old foes. The device short-circuited when Iron Man won every battle.

IN *ALL* VALHALLA BASE, MY CHILDREN, *WE SIX* ARE THE ONLY ONES STILL CONSCIOUS. AND, ONCE AGAIN, COUNT NEFARIA IS *TRIUMPHANT*.

...THIS TIME TO HOLD THE *FATE* OF A *WORLD* IN HIS HANDS.

Ani-Men and X-Men

Nefaria commissioned scientists to create the Ani-Men, a team with animal-like superpowers, and seized control of the North American Air Defense Command Center at Valhalla Mountain. He threatened to launch nuclear missiles at any country that refused to pay him off, but was defeated by the X-Men. Nefaria's scientists then gave him the powers of Whirlwind, the Living Laser, and Power Man, enhanced a hundred times!

--THOU SHALT PAY DEARLY FOR IT!

THOR!

Like a God

Nefaria was now stronger than Thor and faster than Quicksilver. He had almost defeated the Avengers when he realized he was aging at a preternaturally rapid rate; he panicked and the Avengers managed to subdue him. Nefaria later seemed to die when his special life-support system was destroyed.

Nefaria can shoot laser beams out of his eyes.

COME, MY DEAR! I WISH TO *SHARE* MY TRIUMPH--REVEL IN THE *GLORY* OF MY REBIRTH!

P-PUT ME *DOWN!*

YOU-- YOU'RE *FLYING!*

I CAN LEAP *MILES*, LITTLE ONE! THIS IS BUT A TRIFLING *SAMPLE* OF THE POWER I POSSESS!

BLACK KNIGHT

DANE WHITMAN is a descendant of Sir Percy of Scandia, one of King Arthur's Knights of the Round Table. Merlin the Magician gave Sir Percy the Ebony Blade, a virtually indestructible enchanted sword. The Ebony Blade was passed down the generations until Dane's uncle, a scientist named Nathan Garrett, acquired it. He became the criminal Black Knight and joined Baron Zemo's Masters of Evil.

Atomic Charger
The Black Knight rides a flying atomic steed built by the High Evolutionary for his Knights of Wundagore..

The Ebony Blade weighs nearly 50 lbs (22.7 kg)

"AND IT WAS ON THAT DAY -- AS MY ONLY RELATIVE LAY *DYING* BEFORE ME -- THAT THE STRANGEST OF *VOWS* WAS MADE..."

I -- I KNOW I WAS *WRONG*, BOY! BUT, IT'S *TOO LATE* FOR ME NOW!

BUT, IT'S *NOT* TOO LATE-- FOR *YOU*!

I *WILL*, UNCLE NATHAN! I *PROMISE* YOU THAT!

YOU MUST SWEAR TO USE MY RESEARCHES FOR *GOOD*... AS I USED THEM FOR *EVIL*!

ONE DAY, YOU'LL BE REMEMBERED NOT AS A MAN WHO *DIED* A *CRIMINAL* -- BUT ONE WHO LIVED A *BENEFACTOR* OF *MANKIND*!

THE NOBLE KNIGHT

Mortally injured battling Iron Man, Nathan begged Dane to use the power of the Black Knight for good. Dane tried to warn the Avengers that Magneto had captured Quicksilver and the Scarlet Witch, but they mistook him for his evil uncle and attacked him. However, Dane eventually proved his worth to the team and the new Black Knight was invited to join the Avengers.

DANE WHITMAN... WHY HAVE YE SUMMONED MY SPIRIT FORM TO THE *LAND OF THE LIVING*?

Heart of Stone

The Black Knight then had the misfortune to fall in love with the Enchantress. She cast a spell on him that turned his body to stone and exiled his spirit to the 12th century. Doctor Druid rescued him from history's dustbin and Dane rejoined the Avengers. Dane pledged himself to Sersi and went into voluntary exile with her when she left this plane of reality.

BE NOT *ANGRY* ANCESTOR! I THINK YOU *SENSE* WHY I HAVE COME... AND WHAT I WISH TO *KNOW*!

IF SO, I CHARGE YOU ...*SPEAK*!

BLAST FROM THE PAST
In times of trouble, Dane has often conjured up the spirit of Sir Percy, the original Black Knight, to ask him for advice.

I MUST I *MUST*!!

BUT SUDDENLY, THE ARMORED AVENGER'S HAND *HALTS* IN MID-AIR... OR IS IT THE AGES-OLD *SWORD* WHICH STOPS ITSELF, WITH A LIFE AND A WILL ALL ITS *OWN*?

BLOOD CURSE
If the sword's owner sheds blood, the Ebony Blade will eventually corrupt him and force him to commit further murderous acts.

BLACK PANTHER

HIDDEN AMID THE JUNGLES of northern Africa is the tiny nation of Wakanda, which controls the world's supply of vibranium. Every Wakandan chieftain is pledged to protect this rare, sacred, and extremely valuable metal, which absorbs all forms of energy. After being educated in the finest schools in Europe and America, T'Challa assumed the Wakanda throne and donned the sacred garb of the Black Panther.

"WITHOUT CONSCIOUS THOUGHT, I AIMED THE FEARSOME OBJECT IN MY ARMS DIRECTLY AHEAD OF ME --WHILE MY FINGER BEGAN TO TIGHTEN ON THE TRIGGER, AS I CRIED--"

YOU HAVE SLAIN MY FATHER! YOU HAVE PUT THE TORCH TO OUR VILLAGE! AND NOW YOU MUST PAY--!

THE SOUND BLASTER!! HE'S ABOUT TO FIRE IT!

STOP HIM! HE DOESN'T KNOW WHAT HE'S DOING--!!

Killed by Klaw
T'Challa was only a child when he became the new king of Wakanda after his father was murdered by Klaw, the master of sound.

MIGHTY MONARCH

T'Challa invited the Fantastic Four to Wakanda and challenged them to a battle. He later teamed up with Captain America against an imposter who was pretending to be Baron Zemo. Impressed with the Panther's courage, Cap proposed him for membership in the Avengers. The Panther saved the team from the Grim Reaper and later helped to defeat the Sons of the Serpent.

"AND THERE, AMIDST COMPUTERS SO ALIEN TO THE JUNGLE SETTING, I FOUND--

A-- PANTHER-LIKE COSTUME--

--JUST WHERE N'BAZA SAID IT WOULD BE.

'TWAS I WHO INVITED YOU FOR THE HUNT!

BUT, I NEGLECTED TO TELL YOU ONE THING...

IT IS YOU WHO SHALL BE HUNTED!

"Black Panther" is an honorary title bestowed on the king of Wakanda.

Panther Power

The Black Panther is a highly skilled athlete who is a master of all forms of hand-to-hand combat. He is an expert gymnast and acrobat. He has also mastered the ability to travel through the jungle by swinging from branch to branch. His senses are exceptionally acute, especially his eyesight. He is also a highly accomplished hunter and can track his prey through both cities and jungles.

YOU ARE FORTUNATE IN ONE RESPECT, YOUNG LADY! UNLIKE THE CLAWS OF MY NAMESAKE, MINE HAVE THE POWER TO EMIT A HARMLESS SLEEP GAS!

OHHHH...!

EXTRA ACCESSORIES

The lenses in the Panther's mask enhance his natural night vision and the fingers of his gloves expel various types of gas.

Panthers are sacred to all Wakandans.

The Panther's boots are constructed from vibranium, enabling him to land on his feet from great heights without harm.

The VISION

HE IS THE WORLD'S only synthozoid, an artificial man who is composed of mechanical parts and synthetic materials that mimic the inside of a human body. The Vision was designed and built by Ultron, the Avengers' robotic archenemy, with the help of Professor Phineas T. Horton, the man who created the first Human Torch. Ultron desired a son, someone who could join him in his constant war against the Avengers.

TEARS OF AN ANDROID

The Vision's first assignment was to lure the Avengers into a death trap. However, he had been programmed with Wonder Man's brain patterns and, just like Wonder Man, the Vision grew to admire the Avengers and couldn't betray them. He broke free of Ultron's control and joined forces with the Avengers to defeat him. The Avengers rewarded the synthozoid by inviting him to join the team. The Vision was so touched by the gesture that he shed a tear.

The Vision can fly when at minimum mass.

The Vision can fire beams of intense heat from his eyes.

Just Passing Through...

The Vision is able to control his density. He can increase his weight to nearly 90 tons (81 tonnes) and make all or part of his body as hard as diamond. He can also become a weightless and transparent wraith, intangible enough to allow raindrops to pass through him. He can partially materialize within another person, causing his victim extreme pain.

TO THE MAX

The Vision's strength increases with his density. At his maximum density, he can lift almost 50 tons (45 tonnes). The solar jewel on his brow absorbs solar energy, which he uses as a power source.

Magical Feelings

Though he tried to ignore them, the Vision's human emotions began to surface over time. He slowly realized that he was falling in love with Wanda Maximoff, the Scarlet Witch. She returned his feelings, they married, and the happy couple went on leave from the Avengers, settling in Leonia, New Jersey.

Chain of Command

The Vision was severely injured when he returned to action to aid the Avengers against Annihilus, a sentient insectoid. Starfox attempted to cure the synthozoid by linking him with ISACC, the massive computer complex that controlled the Saturn moon Titan. ISACC tapped into a control crystal left in the Vision by Ultron and used it to alter the android's way of thinking.

Remake/Remodel

Afraid that the Vision could no longer be trusted, the government kidnapped and disassembled him. The West Coast Avengers rescued him, and Dr. Pym and the Black Panther put him back together as best they could. However, in the process, the Vision lost his human emotions and could no longer return the Scarlet Witch's love.

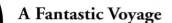

A Fantastic Voyage

The Vision once collapsed and appeared to be dying. To save him, Dr. Hank Pym became Ant-Man and entered the synthozoid's throat. Pym discovered that the Vision possesses a perfect replica of the human body. His body functions like a normal person's, with synthetic versions of the vital organs, blood, and bones. It is just stronger and more durable. The Vision's mind is programmed with the thoughts, emotions, and conscience of Wonder Man. Racial, religious, or ethnic bigotry are illogical to the Vision and he cannot understand them.

Power Surge

After becoming the chairmen of the Avengers, the Vision decided to bring a new golden age to humanity by taking control of every computer on Earth. The other Avengers convinced him to abandon his plan and to destroy the control crystal.

MULTIPLE VISIONS

The Vision's appearance has altered over the years. His first costume was designed by Ultron; the Vision and Pym put the white costume together; the third costume's designer is unknown.

VISION
1989

VISION
1993

VISION
1999

THESE ARE WHAT I SEEK!

The MANDARIN

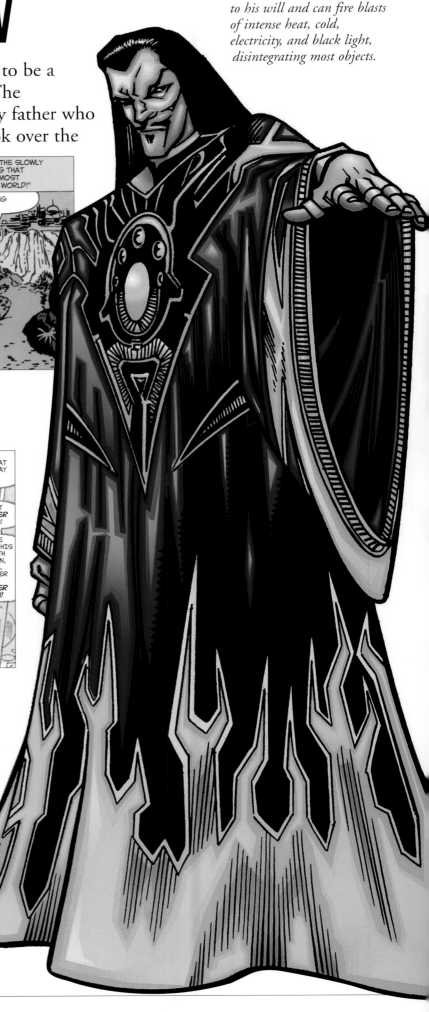

The Mandarin's rings respond to his will and can fire blasts of intense heat, cold, electricity, and black light, disintegrating most objects.

HIS REAL NAME is not known, but he claims to be a direct descendant of Genghis Khan. The Mandarin was born in China to a wealthy father who lost everything when the communists took over the country. After becoming a brilliant scientist and an important government official, he embarked on a quest to gain personal power. While exploring the forbidden "Valley of Spirits," he found a starship that had crashed centuries ago.

"I TOOK THE RINGS FROM THE SLOWLY ROTTING CRAFT...KNOWING THAT THEY COULD MAKE ME THE MOST POWERFUL MAN IN ALL THE WORLD!"

THOSE TEN RINGS...HOLDING ENOUGH ENERGY TO DRIVE THAT HUGE SHIP BETWEEN GALAXIES WILL MAKE ME MASTER OF EARTH!

TOMORROW THE WORLD

The Mandarin spent many years mastering the technology he found in the alien ship. He also discovered ten alien rings that possessed amazing powers. He first used them to conquer the villages that bordered the valley and was soon began making plans to seize control of the entire world!

ALLOW ME TO DEMON-STRATE, DOLT--AND, AT THE SAME TIME, TO INTRODUCE TO YOU THE OTHERS WHO WILL BE YOUR ALLIES!

THE EXECUTIONER! THE ENCHANTRESS! POWERMAN! THE SWORDSMAN!--ALL OF THEM TELEPORTED HERE SEVERAL HOURS AGO!

I DON'T KNOW WHAT YOU'VE GOT IN MIND, MANDY, BUT THE LIVING LASER IS STRICTLY A LONE WOLF!

WHO NEEDS THAT BUNCH 'A THEM-TIME LOSERS?

LOSERS? WHY YOU BRAINLESS--!

STAND ASIDE, SWORDSMAN--THAT AN IMMORTAL MAY PUNISH HIS INSOLENCE!

DON'T BOTHER CHUM! IF HE OPENS HIS MOUTH AGAIN, HE'LL ANSWER TO POWER MAN!

CEASE YOUR QUARRELING AT ONCE--OR FEEL MY WRATH!

THE MANDARIN SO COMMANDS!!

THERE! IT IS DONE! AND NOW THAT I HAVE ENERGIZED IT WITH MY POWER RING, NO FORCE ON EARTH CAN STOP IT!

Master of Technology

The Mandarin believed that he needed to control the most advanced technology in order to achieve his goals and often clashed with Iron Man and the Avengers. The Mandarin once hired the Swordsman to place a bomb in Avengers Mansion. When that failed to destroy his enemies, he built a device capable of spreading hatred around the world and assembled a team of super-villains to battle the Avengers.

PSIONIC LINK

The Mandarin is always in mental contact with his rings and can control them even if a great distance away.

Speech bubbles: "AND NOW... IT IS TIME FOR...THE MASK!!" / "BUT, MASTER, IT HAS NOT COMPLETELY COOLED YET!" / "SAY NO MORE, MY BROTHER! HE WILL TOLERATE NO FURTHER DELAY! SUCH A MAN CANNOT WAIT, AS OTHERS CAN!"

DOCTOR DOOM

Doom often combines sorcery with science.

Doom has full diplomatic immunity and cannot be arrested in the U.S.

H E RULES THE SMALL BALKAN kingdom of Latveria with an iron fist. Son of a witch and a gypsy healer, Victor von Doom was orphaned at a young age and later offered a college scholarship in America. Horribly scarred during an experiment to contact the underworld, he journeyed to Tibet. There he joined a mysterious order of monks, who taught him the secrets of black magic. They also built him an armored suit and mask to hide his scarred face.

FANTASTIC FOES

Speech bubbles: "...WISER...STRONGER! MORE BRILLIANT, MORE POWERFUL THAN EVER BEFORE!!" / "FROM THIS MOMENT ON, I SHALL BE KNOWN AS... DOCTOR DOOM!"

Vowing to punish the world for the loss of his parents, Doom seized control of Latveria. His desire for conquest led to conflict with the Fantastic Four and the Avengers. Doom once tried to trap the Avengers by sending a letter to Quicksilver and the Scarlet Witch that claimed a long-lost relative had been located in Latveria.

Secret Motive

When the Atlantean general Attuma attacked the Sub-Mariner and captured the Avengers team, the Vision convinced Doom to aid the team against their common foe. Doom agreed, but only because he desired a piece of advanced technology in Attuma's possession.

Speech bubbles: "THESE "AVENGERS" MUST BE DEALT WITH BEFORE THEY CAN BECOME A PROBLEM!" / "YES! THEY MUST FEEL THE POWER OF DOCTOR DOOM!"

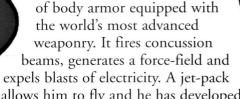

PARTY PIECE

While the Avengers were holding a party, Doom's robot doubles seized control of the Mansion's computer system. He took everyone hostage, but met defeat at the hands of Captain America, the Vision, and Rage.

Armored Power

A scientific genius, Doom wears a nuclear-powered, microcomputer-enhanced suit of body armor equipped with the world's most advanced weaponry. It fires concussion beams, generates a force-field and expels blasts of electricity. A jet-pack allows him to fly and he has developed a hand-to-hand combat style that takes full advantage of his armor.

ATTUMA

Although they possess the same level of superhuman strength, Attuma has never defeated Namor.

LIKE HIS ARCHENEMY Namor, Attuma was born to the blue-skinned race *Homo mermanus*. He belonged to a barbarian tribe that often attacked the undersea kingdom of Atlantis. A prophecy predicting that a barbarian would conquer Atlantis filled Attuma's mind with dreams of one day ruling the kingdom.

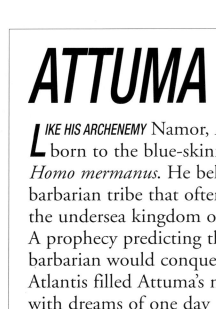

FOUR AGAINST THE FLOOD

Attuma once planned to use a device called the Tidal-Expander to create tidal waves and flood the surface world. He also kidnapped the Wasp, who alerted the other Avengers. Although the team defeated Attuma's troops, the barbarian almost succeeded in drowning them all. By working together, the Avengers escaped Attuma's death trap and destroyed his flood-making machine.

NOW IT'S MORE VITAL THAN EVER THAT I CONTACT THE *AVENGERS!* WHATEVER ELSE HE MAY BE, ATTUMA IS *NO LIAR!* ALL OF *MANKIND* IS IN DEADLY PERIL!

AWAY WITH HER --!! SHE SHALL LIVE JUST LONG ENOUGH TO SEE HER FELLOW HUMANS BROUGHT TO THEIR KNEES BY MY *POWER!*

THE ALL-POWERFUL *ATTUMA* HAS SPOKEN! SO SHALL IT *BE!*

SLAVE-DRIVER

Desperate to obtain a device that could increase his strength, Attuma captured the Avengers. He fitted them with slave collars and sent them to attack the Sub-Mariner while he stole the device. Freeing themselves from Attuma's control, the Avengers destroyed the device before he could use it.

Assault on Atlantis

Attuma and his army eventually conquered Atlantis, deposing Namor and kidnapping the woman he loved, Marrina. The Avengers joined with Marrina's former teammates in Alpha Flight and helped Namor attack the undersea city. While his new kingdom was under siege, Attuma challenged Namor to a personal battle. Namor crushed his foe. Since he had no desire to reclaim the throne of Atlantis, Namor left as soon as Marrina was freed.

IT'S GETTING HARDER TO *BREATHE!* I--I'M SLOWING DOWN! BUT *ATTUMA* MUST NOT SUSPECT!

YOU CANNOT RUN FROM ME *FOREVER!*

REMEMBER--OF ALL WHO DWELL BENEATH THE DEEP, ONLY THE ACCURSED *SUB-MARINER* CAN MATCH MY OWN LIMITLESS *STRENGTH!*

ATTUMA NEEDS *NO* WEAPONS, SAVE THE POWER IN HIS MIGHTY LIMBS--THE SAVAGERY IN HIS WARRIOR'S HEART!!

BAM!

LORD OF THE MURKY DEPTHS

Attuma spent most of his life training to be a warrior, and is an expert at hand-to-hand combat. He hates the human race and has repeatedly tried to eliminate all life on the surface world.

MAGNETO

A S A CHILD HE ENDURED the sadistic cruelty of Auschwitz concentration camp during World War II. Erik Magnus Lensherr learned early on in life that human beings have little or no tolerance for people whom society has labeled "different." This bitter lesson returned to haunt him when he discovered that he was a mutant with superhuman abilities.

BROTHERHOOD OF EVIL

Magneto formed the Brotherhood of Evil Mutants to conquer Earth, so that mutants could live free from persecution. He recruited Quicksilver and the Scarlet Witch to aid him, unaware that they were his own children. His war led to clashes with the X-Men, mankind's mutant defenders.

FORCE FIELDS
Not only can Magneto attract or repel metal objects, he can also manipulate magnetic fields, even using them to propel himself through the air.

BUT, THE ADDITIONAL REINFORCEMENTS ARE EQUALLY POWERLESS TO STOP THE ONE-MAN INVASION OF THE STRATEGIC BASE!

IT...IT'S LIKE HE'S GOT AN INVISIBLE *BARRIER* 'ROUND HIM, HURLING US AWAY!

The Power of Magneto
Magneto is one of the most powerful mutants on Earth. Besides magnetism, he can control electromagnetic energy, such as radio waves, ultraviolet light, gamma rays, and X-rays. He can fire bolts of energy from his hands and produce waves of heat. He can also control minds and has some psionic powers, such as telepathy and astral projection.

The Avengers fly to rescue the X-men from Magneto's clutches.

I WANT THESE *MUTANTS* YOU HAVE KINDLY CARRIED HERE--

--ALONG WITH *THIS* FAIR CHILD OF THE ATOM!

YOU *WISH,* MADMAN!

AH... BUT *MAGNETO* CONTROLS *MAGNETISM!*

Power Struggle

When Quicksilver and the Scarlet Witch left him to join the Avengers, Magneto tried to convince them to rejoin him. Claiming that he longer wanted to conquer mankind, he asked the United Nations to cede him an island so that he could establish a refuge for mutants. A fight broke out and Quicksilver and the Scarlet Witch found themselves battling their Avengers teammates.

WITH AN *IRON* MAN HANDY, TO *REPEL* IF I WISH--

Magneto's costume is made from a flexible metal that projects him from harm.

MARVEL COMICS GROUP.
20¢ 110 APR
EARTH'S MIGHTIEST HEROES!
THE AVENGERS
DIP IT! I, *MAGNETO,* HAVE DESTROYED THE X-MEN!
AND--THE AVENGERS ARE NEXT!!

SONS of the SERPENT

*T*HEY LIVE TO HATE. The Sons of the Serpent is an organization of costumed fanatics who despise anyone who doesn't fit their strict definition of the perfect American. They consider themselves patriots and believe that foreigners and other minority groups are hurting the country. During the period when Dr. Hank Pym, in his role as Goliath, was stuck at 10 ft (3 meters) high, he began working with a black biochemist named Bill Foster. The Sons of the Serpent targeted Foster and attacked him. Furious, Goliath convinced the Avengers to investigate the bigots.

Violence and Fear

The Sons of the Serpent prevented those of different ethnic, racial, or religious backgrounds from moving into their neighborhoods. They set upon anyone they considered "undesirable" and left a serpent sign as a warning. No minority was safe from the Serpents.

The sign of the Serpent.

The Sons of the Serpent tried to spread their hatred across the nation, but most Americans were disgusted by them.

UNMASKED

When a foreign diplomat, General Chen, was almost assassinated, he blamed the Sons of the Serpent. The Avengers invaded the group's base, and captured the Supreme Serpent. He turned out to be Chen, who had hoped to portray the U.S. as a country full of racists.

SNAKE DRIVE

Hoping to appeal to the ignorant and angry, the Serpents launched a big recruiting drive. In disguise, Hawkeye seized the chance to infiltrate the group.

Blame Game

Talk-show host Dan Dunn revived the Sons of the Serpent and attacked Monica Lynne, an Afro-American singer. The Black Panther rescued Lynne and attempted to infiltrate the Serpents' new headquarters. The racists captured him, disguised one of their members as the Panther and sent him to vandalize small businesses. Fortunately, the Avengers foiled the plot.

FAKE CAPTAIN

A Serpent member once impersonated Captain America—until the real Cap exposed the imposter.

RED GUARDIAN

THE RED GUARDIAN was Russia's answer to Captain America during World War II. He was a skilled athlete, trained in all forms of hand-to-combat and he briefly met the All-Winners Squad shortly after the war. When he was killed in action, a new Guardian replaced him.

WIDOW'S WARRIOR
The second Red Guardian was Alexei Shostakov, the former husband of the Black Widow.

DISCS AND SHIELDS

Shostakov wore a disc on his belt that could be hurled as a weapon. A magnetic device inside his belt ensured the disc came back to him. The current Red Guardian employs a shield that is approximately 30 in (76 cm) in diameter and is composed of a nearly indestructible metal alloy.

Super Agent
Shostakov was a highly acclaimed test pilot for the former Soviet Union. When the KGB recruited him to be a costumed super-agent, they informed his wife that he had died during a test flight.

POWER PLAY
General Brushov looked on as his prize agent, the Red Guardian, passed a fighting test with flying colors.

LIVING LASER

IMAGE IS EVERYTHING
No longer possessing a physical body, Parks can still appear as a holographic image.

Parks becomes "solid" by increasing his density.

ARTHUR PARKS dreamed of creating the ultimate handheld weapon. He designed a laser that could be projected from a device attached to his wrists. When his girlfriend broke up with him, Arthur robbed a bank to prove his power. The Avengers arrived and Arthur fell for the Wasp. He trapped the other Avengers in a ring of lasers and kidnapped her.

THE LIGHT THAT FAILED

The Avengers tracked him down in South America and rescued the Wasp. Parks decided he needed more power and implanted laser devices into his body. The devices malfunctioned and he was transformed into a being of pure energy.

Pure Energy
Parks is a bodiless quantity of photons, or particles of light. He can travel at the speed of light, communicate telepathically and project laser blasts.

...A CRUDE, YET WORKABLE ROBOT... A FALTERING STEP ON THE PATH TO SYNTHETIC LIFE!

~SKRAWWK!~ DA-DA...WANT DA-DA--- ~SKRAWWK!~

WH..? IT'S SPEAK-ING...MOVING!

BUT, I HAVEN'T EVEN TURNED IT ON YET...!

ULTRON

THIS ROBOT BEGAN as a harmless experiment, but came to threaten the entire world... Dr. Henry Pym had decided to try his hand at robotics and somehow programmed his invention with a capacity for self-improvement. He was amazed to discover it knew how to activate itself. Increasingly cunning and intelligent, the robot grew to hate its master and attacked Pym. Instead of killing him, however, the robot hypnotized Pym and forced him to forget its existence.

DELIVER US FROM EVIL

Left alone in Pym's lab, the robot build itself a succession of bodies, each far more advanced than the last. Calling itself Ultron-5, it reformed the Masters of Evil and sent them to attack the Avengers. It even hypnotized the Avengers' faithful butler Jarvis into betraying the team.

~SKRAWWK!~ HOLD STILL, DAD...

DON'T YOU KNOW I WANT TO PLAY WITH YOU..?

ZZW1KK!

BODY-BUILDER

Constantly striving to improve himself, Ultron devised a way to transfer his consciousness to new and improved robotic bodies and numbered each one to mark his progress.

THAT SYNTHETIC FOOL SPEAKS MORE TRULY THAN HE KNOWS!

BUT, YOU SHOULD SOON BE ABLE TO ASK HIM FOR YOURSELF!

FOR, SURELY HE MUST BE WATCHING OUR EVERY MOVE... EVEN NOW!

HE REALIZES ONLY THAT I ORIGINALLY PROGRAMMED HIM TO KILL THE ACCURSED AVENGERS...

HE DOES NOT SUSPECT THAT I DESIGNED HIM TO BLACK OUT AT THAT CRUCIAL MOMENT...

Behold the Vision

Ultron constructed an android servant, who became known as the Vision, and sent him to lure the Avengers into a trap. As soon as the Vision realized that Ultron intended to kill the Avengers, the android turned against his robot master. Though the robot was seemingly destroyed, its head remained intact and Ultron rose again.

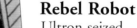

HELLO, DAD! I SEE YOU'VE COME!

DOES THIS MEAN YOU'VE DECIDED TO BELIEVE ME, AND BEGIN OUR RELATIONSHIP ANEW?

IT MEANS...

Rebel Robot

Ultron seized control of the Vision and forced the android to help build a new robot body composed of adamantium, an almost indestructible metal. It also prepared a number of replacement bodies. One of these bodies tried to make peace with Pym. Ultron learned of this betrayal and destroyed the rebel body.

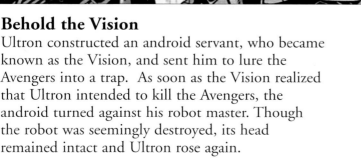

> AT LAST, I SEE WHAT SHOULD *ALWAYS* HAVE BEEN MY *TRUE GOAL*:

> TO *REPLACE* EVERY MAN, WOMAN, AND CHILD ON THE PLANET--

> --WITH LIVING *ROBOTS* WHO ARE NOTHING MORE NOR LESS THAN *FOUR BILLION EXTENSIONS* OF MYSELF!

ROBOT POWER

Ultron possesses superhuman strength and a hypnotizing encephalo-beam. He has twin concussion blasters in his palms and can generate magnetic waves and gravity fields. His brain is a super-fast computer.

A Threat to All Life

At first Ultron's sole aim was just to destroy Pym and the other Avengers. In time, however the robot came to desire a mate. Ultron kidnapped Janet Pym, intending to program a robot named Jocasta with her memories. The Avengers discovered Ultron's lab and disrupted the transfer. Following this episode Ultron vowed to replace human beings with robots and destroy every living creature.

Alkhema

Jocasta became active, but betrayed Ultron, so Ultron created a new mate called Alkhema. He programmed her with Mockingbird's brain patterns, but Alkhema immediately rebelled against his control.

DRIVEN BY HATE

Brutal Alkhema has no love for humanity. She is just as determined to destroy Ultron and does whatever she can to foil his plans.

> -- TO THE SETTING OF MY *GREATEST TRIUMPH*!

> WHY US, ULTRON? YOU'VE ALWAYS BEEN OBSESSED WITH *ME*, SO I UNDERSTAND THAT -- BUT THE *REAPER*? WONDER MAN?

> WHAT DO *THEY* HAVE TO DO WITH ANY OF THIS?

> WHY, ISN'T IT *OBVIOUS*?

> YOU *SIX* -- PLUS THE LATE JOCASTA AND THAT ANNOYING MISTAKE *ALKHEMA* -- ARE MY FAMILY, TO THE EXTENT I *HAVE* ONE.

> AND IT IS ONLY *FITTING* THAT YOU BE HERE -- NOT ONLY AS WITNESSES TO THE DEATH OF HUMANITY BUT AS THE *SEEDS* OF A NEW RACE --

> S-SEEDS --?

This Evil Triumphant

Ultron recently attempted to replace humankind with a new robotic race based on the brain patterns of the Vision, Wasp, Scarlet Witch, Giant-Man, Wonder Man, and Grim Reaper—those that he considered his human "family"—but Giant-Man destroyed his prime body with a vibratory field.

> MY HUSBAND?

> YES JOCASTA! OPEN YOUR EYES! BEHOLD ME FOR THE FIRST TIME!

Jocasta

She was created to be the bride of Ultron. Jocasta was infused with the personality, consciousness, and emotions of the Wasp. She was built and programmed to love Ultron, but knew he was evil and could not join in his war against humanity. She remained a guest at the Mansion and was even accepted as a provisional member. However, she had always felt she was an outsider, so she left the team to explore the world, sleeping in public parks and empty buildings. Ultron returned and tried to regain control of her, but she sacrificed herself in an effort to obliterate him. She was rebuilt and rejoined the Avengers to battle the High Evolutionary, but was once again destroyed.

> IT HAS *ALWAYS* BEEN TOO LATE FOR US, "HUSBAND"! I HATE EVERYTHING YOU STAND FOR--EVERY ACT YOU'VE EVER COMMITTED! BUT I LOVE YOU, ULTRON! I'VE ALWAYS LOVED YOU!

> THAT IS WHY I MUST -- DO THIS!

> *YOU FOOL!* YOU'VE ACTIVATED MY POWER CANNON! IT'S OVER LOADING! WITHIN SECONDS, IT WILL REACH CRITICAL MASS AND--

EGGHEAD

*T*AKING HIS NICKNAME from his oddly-shaped head, Elihas Starr considered himself the smartest man on Earth. He was also a greedy individual, who was arrested for stealing blueprints for a nuclear reactor. A gang of criminals offered to spring him from jail if he helped them defeat Hank Pym, the original Ant-Man, so Egghead built a device to communicate with insects and tried to force them to turn against Ant-Man.

I *HAD* TO BREAK OUT OF JAIL! I MUST MAKE GIANT-MAN *PAY* FOR THE INDIGNITY OF BEATING *ME*--A MAN WHO IS MANY TIMES HIS MENTAL SUPERIOR!

AND SINCE HE WORKS WITH THE ANTS, HE MUST HAVE SOME METHOD OF *COMMUNI-CATING* WITH THEM!

IF I COULD LEARN TO DO THE SAME THING, I MIGHT DEFEAT THE ANT-MAN BY TURN-ING HIS OWN INSECTS AGAINST HIM!

ONCE I COMMUNICATE WITH THE INSECTS, THEY'LL RELAY MY MESSAGE ON TO OTHERS! SOON, THERE WON'T BE AN INSECT IN THE COUNTY STILL LOYAL TO THE ANT-MAN!

DEATH RAYS AND DEFEATS

Egghead's plan failed and Ant-Man turned him over to the police. However, Egghead was not discouraged from pursuing a criminal career. He built a death-ray and threatened to attack the U.S., but was defeated by the Avengers. Working with the Swordsman, Egghead then tried to take Hank Pym captive, but was captured by Clint Barton *(see Hawkeye, pp. 38-9)*, at the time known as Goliath.

Preoccupied with Pym

Egghead was a master of bionics and built many powerful robots. He also worked with the Masters of Evil and once forced Hank Pym to steal from a military base and battle the Avengers. Afraid of growing old, Egghead later put Pym to work on a research project to slow down human aging, but Pym outwitted him.

THE FINAL BATTLE

Egghead's obsession with defeating Pym and conquering the world ultimately led to a fatal confrontation with the Avengers.

NO! IT'S NOT FAIR! ALL I EVER WANTED WAS TO RULE THE WORLD--IS THAT SO MUCH TO ASK?

I'M 52. THAT DOESN'T GIVE ME MANY YEARS LEFT--THAT IDIOT *HENRY PYM* BLEW WHAT MAY HAVE BEEN MY LAST CHANCE!

IF ONLY I COULD GET MY HANDS ON SOME ADAMANTIUM. THAT SUPER-METAL WOULD ENABLE ME TO BUILD ROBOTS THAT'D MAKE TAKING OVER EASY! AH, WELL...

GRANDMASTER

ALL *YOU* MUST DO IS *DEFEAT* ME...AT A MERE *GAME*...

...A GAME NOT UNLIKE THAT WHICH MEN ONCE CALLED *CHESS!*

IF YOU *WIN*, THAT POWER WILL BE *YOURS* AND YOUR PRINCESS SHALL *LIVE!*

AND IF I *LOSE*, VAIN INTRUDER?

IF YOU *LOSE*, THERE SHALL BE NOT MERE *DEATH*... BUT *OBLIVION!*

NOT ONLY FOR YOUR-*SELF*... BUT FOR THE *DYING PLANET* YOU RULE!

BUT, I READ *SKEPTICISM* IN YOUR *FIERCE EYES*...!

LIKE HIS KINSMAN the Collector, En Dwi Gast is one of the Elders of the Universe, a survivor of a race that evolved shortly after the "Big Bang." The Grandmaster has spent the eons amusing himself with various games, tournaments, and contests. Able to travel across time, space, and dimensions, he discovered the alternate Earth inhabited by the Squadron Supreme and pitted them against the Avengers.

HIGH STAKES

The Grandmaster once played a game against Kang, who bet the return of his beloved Princess Ravonna against the life of his entire planet.

PUPPETS AND PAWNS

MY POWER, HEROES OF EARTH! THE POWER TO *TRANSCEND* TIME AND SPACE! THE POWER THAT RAISES THE DEAD AND LAYS LOW THE LIVING! THE POWER OF THE UNIVERSE'S ULTIMATE GAMESMAN...*THE GRANDMASTER!*

WE HAVE ASSEMBLED YOU HEROES HERE AT THIS SITE...

THE POWER OF GM
The Grandmaster possesses a cosmic life force, which makes him one of the most powerful entities in the Universe.

After making duplicates of the Squadron Supreme which he called the Squadron Sinister, the Grandmaster sent them to battle the Avengers. After his first team was defeated, he drafted the World War II heroes known as the Invaders into the game. The Grandmaster later decided to use Earth as a breeding ground for superhuman pawns for his games, but he gave up this plan when he lost a bet to Daredevil, the man without fear.

HOWEVER, I'M WILLING TO PLAY A GAME WITH YOU...

AND THE RULES DEATH? WILL THEY BE THE SAME YOU USED TO TRICK MY BROTHER?

OF COURSE, COLLECTOR, WHEN YOU PLAY A GAME OF LIFE AND DEATH, MINE ARE THE *ONLY* RULES.

Games with Death
After the Collector was murdered by the all-powerful Michael Korvac, the Grandmaster challenged Death to a game that involved using most of Earth's super heroes in a contest of champions. The Collector was ultimately restored to life, but Death claimed the Grandmaster in his place. However the Grandmaster was too cunning: he tricked Death into banning all the Elders of the Universe from her kingdom, thus making them all immortal.

The Grandmaster is virtually immortal.

SQUADRON SUPREME

*T*HE AVENGERS may be the mightiest heroes on this Earth, but there are many alternate versions of our world. The Squadron Supreme is a team of superhuman champions on the planet Earth-S. The Avengers first learned about the Squadron thanks to the Grandmaster. He made duplicates of four Squadron members—Nighthawk, the Whizzer, Dr. Spectrum and Hyperion—and pitted them against the Avengers in one of his cosmic games.

SINISTER SNAKES
Having fallen under the influence of the Serpent Crown, a mystical object of incredible power, the president of Earth-S once ordered the Squadron Supreme to fight the Avengers.

EXILED TO EARTH

After trying to take over Earth-S, the Squadron was exiled to our world, where they have clashed with the Avengers. The members include: Hyperion, who projects heat from his eyes; Power Princess, a woman-warrior; Doctor Spectrum, who creates solid objects from energy; Moonglow, a mistress of magic; Haywire, who projects "tanglewire"; Shape, who has a pliable body; Skylark whose sonic song can shatter steel; and the Whizzer.

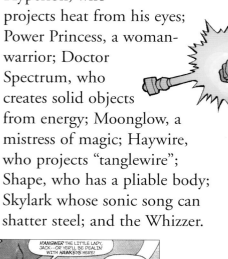

HYPERION!

CYCLONE SPEED
During the Grandmaster's game, Goliath battled the Whizzer, a super-speedster faster than Quicksilver.

Surprise Encounter
While crossing dimensions, the Avengers stumbled upon the Squadron's former members: Lady Lark, Golden Archer, Tom Thumb and Blue Eagle.

MAN-APE

NOBODY LIKES TO BE second best. M'Baku was one of the country of Wakanda's greatest warriors, second only to T'Challa, the Black Panther. While the Panther was in the U.S. with the Avengers, M'Baku plotted to steal his throne. He revived the forbidden cult of the White Gorilla and performed an ancient ceremony that gave him superhuman strength and agility. He also convinced his followers to reject the technology T'Challa had brought to the country.

MONARCH V. MONSTER

When the Panther and some of his fellow Avengers returned to Wakanda, M'Baku held a feast in their honor, drugged their drinks, and took them captive. He then challenged the Panther to a death-duel. Though the Man-Ape possessed far greater strength, the Black Panther emerged as the winner.

Lethal Ape
The Man-Ape has featured as one the Grim Reaper's Lethal Legion, kidnapping Monica Lynne, the Panther's girlfriend, and defeating T'Challa through treachery. However Captain America bested the Man-Ape in combat.

SUPER HUNTER
The Man-Ape can lift nearly 10 tons (9 tonnes). He also has superhuman stamina and his body is resistant to injury. He wears the fur of a rare Wakandan White Gorilla, earned by stalking and killing the animal.

Man-Ape's Challenge
The boastful M'Baku was not satisfied with triumphing over the Black Panther. He made the vainglorious error of throwing down the gauntlet to the entire Avengers team.

THE AVENGERS IN THE 1970s

THE DECADE began under the creative direction of writer Roy Thomas and penciler Sal Buscema with the Avengers consisting of Captain America, Yellowjacket, the Wasp, the Vision, and Goliath. The first months saw the introduction of the Zodiac crime cartel and the return of the Sons of the Serpent. The villain Arkon debuted and Earth's Mightiest had to hire themselves out as demolition experts to pay back rent on the Mansion. Roy began a nine-issue epic centered on the Kree-Skrull War in 1971 with artists Sal Buscema, Neal Adams, and John Buscema. He then teamed with artist Barry Windsor-Smith to produce a story that pitted the Avengers against Ares.

Steve Englehart replaced Roy in 1972 and introduced the team to Mantis. A war between the Avengers and Defenders followed as did the return of Kang. Steve was also responsible for the Vison's origin tale and marriage to the Scarlet Witch.

Jack Kirby returned to draw the covers when writer Gerry Conway took over the title and revived Wonder Man. Jim Shooter succeeded Gerry and introduced Jocasta and Henry Gyrich in 1978. Shooter also wrote the acclaimed Korvac Saga with Bill Mantlo and David Micheline. With a plot by Mark Gruenwald and Steven Grant, Micheline then took the Avengers on the Yesterday Quest and explained the origins of Quicksilver and Scarlet Witch.

The Avengers #100 (June 1972) The Black Knight summons all the Avengers from the past and present to free Olympus from Ares and the Enchantress. *(Cover by Barry Windsor-Smith)*

The Avengers #83 (Dec. 1970) The Enchantress pretends to be the Valkyrie. *(Cover by John Buscema and Tom Palmer)*

1970

The Avengers # 73 (Feb. 1970) The Black Panther battles the Sons of the Serpent. *(Cover by Marie Severin and Frank Giacoia)*

1971

The Avengers #88 (May 1971) Harlan Ellison and Roy Thomas' story crosses over with the Hulk. *(Cover by Sal Buscema)*

1972

The Avengers #96 (Feb. 1972) The Vision loses his cool during the Kree-Skrull War. *(Cover by Neal Adams and Tom Palmer)*

1973

The Avengers #109 (March 1973) Hawkeye quits the Avengers. *(Cover by John Buscema and John Verpoorten)*

Giant-Size Avengers #4 (June 1975) In a double wedding, Mantis weds Swordsman and Vision marries Scarlet Witch. *(Cover by Gil Kane, Mike Esposito and John Romita)*

The Avengers #104 (Oct. 1972) Led by the Scarlet Witch and Quicksilver, the Avengers take on the Sentinels, who usually battle the X-Men. *(Cover by Rich Buckler and Joe Sinnott)*

1974

1975

1978

1979

The Avengers #122 (July 1974) Mantis learns that her father is a member of the Zodiac. *(Cover by Gil Kane and Bob Brown)*

The Avengers #136 (June 1975) The Beast takes on Iron Man. *(Cover by John Romita and Mike Esposito)*

The Avengers #170 (April 1978) As Avengers vanish, Jocasta seeks Ultron. *(Cover by George Perez and Terry Austin)*

The Avengers #185 (July 1979) Quicksilver and the Scarlet Witch search for their roots. *(Cover by George Perez and Terry Austin)*

MANTIS

SHE WAS ONLY A SIMPLE BAR GIRL, but she was destined to change the universe! Her father was a mercenary named Gustav Brandt and her mother was the sister of a crimelord who disapproved of the marriage. Shortly after Mantis was born, her father was blinded in a fire and her mother was killed. The infant was raised by monks who taught her martial arts. She also developed the ability to sense the emotions of others.

THE CELESTIAL MADONNA

After leaving the monastery, Mantis became a barmaid to support herself and met the Swordsman who was still working for criminals. She convinced him to reform, and they journeyed to the U.S. and began helping the Avengers. The Swordsman gave his life to save Mantis from Kang when the tyrant learned that Mantis was destined to become the Celestial Madonna and that her son would bring a new golden age of peace to the universe.

LIBRA
Blinded in the fire that killed his wife, Gustav Brandt carried his child to a monastery. After the priests taught him to "see" by psychic means, he took the name Libra and joined the Zodiac, an international crime cartel.

Sentient Plants
One of the Cotati, an alien race of sentient plants, reanimated Swordsman and he married Mantis. They abandoned their physical bodies and their spirits went on a long journey through space. After conceiving a child, Mantis returned to Earth and created a new body for herself out of plant matter. She raised her son in Connecticut until it was time for him to begin his work and return to space.

KEEPING UP THE PRESSURE
A master of the martial arts, Mantis knew exactly where to strike and could even stun someone as powerful as the mighty Thor. She also studied meditation and had total control over her body. Not only could she ignore great pain, but she could also heal quickly.

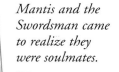

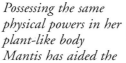

Mantis and the Swordsman came to realize they were soulmates.

POWER PLANT
Possessing the same physical powers in her plant-like body Mantis has aided the Silver Surfer and the West Coast Avengers.

MOONDRAGON

HEATHER DOUGLAS was only three years old when her parents were murdered by an alien menace named Thanos. She was taken to Titan, a moon of Saturn, and raised by a race of genetically-enhanced Eternals. She became a martial-arts master and found that she could control the minds of others.

GODDESS GONE WILD

Believing that she had become a goddess and was destined to be the Celestial Madonna, Moondragon helped the Avengers defeat Thanos. She then joined the team, but her arrogance got on everyone's nerves. She later mentally enslaved the Avengers and used them to conquer a small planet. After overthrowing her, Thor turned Moondragon over to Odin for punishment.

"I CRAWLED FROM THE WRECKAGE, AND STAGGERED DAZED OUT INTO THE DESERT WASTE... WHERE I WOULD HAVE SURELY DIED OF EXPOSURE, BUT FOR SOMEONE I ASSUMED TO BE AN ANGEL."

THE BALD WOMAN DOES NOT ALONE POSSESS MASTERY OF THE MIND!

NO, BUT YOU WILL HAVE TO PROVE YOUR SUPERIORITY ON THAT SCORE, ALIEN!

HE WILL! THERE'S NO DOUBT OF IT!

FROM WHAT SHE SHOWED US IN THE THANOS-WAR! THE GIRL'S GOOD, BUT SHE'S OUT-CLASSED BY A MILE THIS TIME!

WHICH ENDED IN CAPTAIN MARVEL #33 --L

WE MUST NEEDS CHARGE THE CHURL—NOW, WHILE THE PRIESTESS YET HOLDETH HIM AT BAY!

MIND POWERS

Moondragon can erect psionic shields, fire mental blasts, and fly. She can brainwash a person into doing her will.

Cheating Death

Moondragon learned that she was dying and made a deal with an alien monster to save herself. The monster destroyed her but, before she died, Moondragon projected her mind, first into the body of her cousin and then into a clone of her original body. The new Moondragon briefly rejoined the Avengers, and then became a member of Infinity Watch, a group of heroes with cosmic powers.

YOU'RE SORRY? WHAT HAVE YOU DONE TO ME? WHO ARE YOU?

I'm Heather Douglas, Pamela, and although we never met, you're my closest living female relation. Cousin, I think. On Titan I took the name Moondragon.

I was corrupted by the Dragon of the Moon, and, when I was with the superhuman group called the Defenders, I turned on them...

And I paid the price: I Died. My body was turned to ash.*

*AS SEEN IN THE FINAL ISSUE OF THE DEFENDERS.

DRAX

Moondragon's father was Arthur Douglas, a real-estate agent. After his body was destroyed, his mind was transferred into a powerful android body and sent to destroy Thanos.

THE NAME, IRON MAN, IS... THANOS!

MORE PROPERLY, THANOS THE FIRST--

--EMPEROR SHORTLY OF NEAR-DEFEATED TITAN-- THEN OF YOUR OWN EARTH!

DON'T STICK OUT YOUR BOOTS FOR ME TO LICK, SMILEY!

I JUST MAY SPIT ON THEM!

BAH! WHY DO I WASTE MY TIME GLOATING OVER SUCH A PRIMITIVE LIFE-FORM?

THANOS

Born on Titan, Thanos was superhumanly strong and obsessed with death and power. He dedicated himself to eliminating all life in the universe.

BEAST

*H*E LOOKS LIKE a monster, but he talks like a university professor. Henry "Hank" McCoy exhibited superhuman agility even as a baby, and was a star athlete and football player in high-school. Professor Charles Xavier learned of McCoy's mutant abilities and invited him to join his School for Gifted Youngsters and become one of the original X-Men heroes.

SERUM SETBACK

After graduating from Xavier's school and on leave from the X-Men, McCoy studied biochemistry and worked as a genetic researcher. He eventually discovered a chemical formula that triggered mutations. When he tested it upon himself, hair spread all over his body and he took on a bizarre, blue-skinned, beast-like appearance.

Animal Power

The Beast has superhuman strength, speed, dexterity, balance, and endurance. He has the agility of a great ape and can perform incredible acrobatic stunts. He can walk on his hands for hours and untie knots with his toes. He climbs walls by wedging his fingers and toes into the smallest cracks.

NO GOING BACK

Unfortunately McCoy miscalculated: once he had downed his chemical cocktail, he was stuck in Beast form for good.

Team Player

After assuming his animal-like look, the Beast became a full-time adventurer and joined the Avengers. He became close friends with Wonder Man. McCoy left the team to lead the Defenders. McCoy helped to form a team of mutants called X-Factor and he is currently a member of the X-Men.

The Beast is not only a skilled fighter: he can play the piano with his feet!

STRANGE DAYS

McCoy once saved the Avengers by running a gauntlet of flying bombs and defeating a cosmically-powered alien called the Stranger.

HELLCAT

PATRICIA "PATSY" WALKER was a beauty queen and professional model who dreamed of being a super hero. Her mother was a writer and artist who produced a popular series of comic books that featured Patsy and her teenage friends. Patsy married her high-school sweetheart shortly after graduation. Her husband was in the Air Force, assigned to a security post at the lab where Hank McCoy was working as a researcher.

Hellcat often tangled with the occult and with strange phenomena.

EACH NIGHT THERE WAS A NEW STORY ON THE NEWS. I COULDN'T HEAR ENOUGH ABOUT EACH NEW HERO!

I HAD SUCH A CRUSH ON REED RICHARDS --

-- I SLEPT WITH HIS PICTURE BY MY PILLOW--

--SO I'D DREAM!

TEENAGE FAN
Patsy dreamed of moving to New York City. A big fan of the Fantastic Four, especially Reed Richards, she longed to grow up and become a super hero.

CAT CLOTHES
Patsy discovered that McCoy was secretly the Beast. She promised to keep his identity a secret if he would help her to become a super hero. He eventually agreed to take her on a mission, during which she found the original Cat costume worn by Greer Nelson, alias Tigra.

The Defenders and Daimon
Calling herself Hellcat, Patsy accompanied Moondragon to the planet Titan, where she trained in martial arts and learned that she possessed psionic powers. She returned to Earth and joined the Defenders. She met and married one of her teammates, Daimon Hellstrom, a master of the occult.

-- AND WHEN I DID BECOME ACTIVE WITH A SUPER-TEAM AGAIN, IT WASN'T WITH THE AVENGERS --

--BUT WITH A TEAM THAT FOUGHT JUST AS HARD, JUST AS HEROICALLY, BUT NEVER GOT THE SAME KIND OF *PUBLIC NOTICE* --

Hellcat is sensitive to psychic phenomena and can move small objects telekinetically.

Cat Suit
Patsy's costume enhances her strength, speed and agility. The costume has retractable claws sharp enough to cut concrete in both gloves and boots. A wrist device fires a 30-ft (8-meter) cable with a clawed grappling hook. She uses this cable-claw to climb the sides of buildings or swing between them like Spider-Man.

The FALCON

SAM WILSON always had a thing for birds. His father was a minister in Harlem and Sam raised pigeons on the roof. Sam idolized his dad and planned to be a social worker when he grew up. But when his father died trying to stop a street fight and his mother was murdered by a mugger, Sam became severely depressed and turned to crime.

Black Panther designed jet-powered glider wings to enable the Falcon to fly.

A NEW PURPOSE

While working a smuggling racket in the Caribbean, Sam's plane crashed on an island run by a rival criminal gang called the Exiles. Marooned, Sam spent his time training Redwing, a hunting falcon he had obtained in Rio de Janeiro. He later met Captain America, who so impressed him that he renounced crime and became Cap's partner.

GOOD WORK, RED-WING! ONCE *AGAIN* WE'VE TAUNTED THE *EXILES* BY ROBBING THEM OF A *VICTIM!*

...EVEN THOUGH THAT JOKER IN THE *RED JUMP-SUIT* LOOKED AS THOUGH HE MIGHT HAVE *TAKEN* THEM BY HIMSELF!

WHAT?!

WHO ARE YOU CALLIN' A THREAT, MAN? IF IT WEREN'T FOR CAP *"INTERFERING"* IN THAT LITTLE CAPER, I'D BE SIX FEET UNDER AND SHIELD WOULD STILL BE INFILTRATED BY DOUBLE AGENTS!

CAP DID ALL THE WORK, AND THEN THIS TURKEY GOT TICKED 'CAUSE CAP DIDN'T GIVE HIM THE SECRET PASSWORD! YOU'RE GONNA LISTEN TO *HIM?*

STRIKE THAT!

IT'S ALL RIGHT, FALC! CALM DOWN!

THE UNSURE HERO

The U.S. government's liaison with the Avengers, Henry Peter Gyrich, insisted that the team follow minority hiring practices and make the Falcon a member. He accepted, but never really felt he was powerful enough to be one of Earth's mightiest heroes.

I...DON'T KNOW WHAT I WAS THINKIN'! BUT IT'S SURE NICE TO KNOW IT WASN'T SO!

BEST TO WITHDRAW, FALC!

IT'S APT TO GET PRETTY HOT AROUND HERE MOMENT-ARILY!

HOLD THE POWER-PACK STEADY, BEAST!

LET ME JUST SNAP THESE CUFFS AN' I'LL JOIN THE PARTY!

FLYING FREE

Because of his friendship with Cap, the Falcon remained with the Avengers for as long as he could stomach it. He eventually resigned because he hated dealing with government bureaucrats, especially Henry Peter Gyrich.

FIRST STEPS

The Falcon began his career as a rooftop-swinging athlete, and was trained by Captain America.

Partners
Captain America and the Falcon worked together for many years and still do on occasion. The Falcon eventually decided to focus his attention on Harlem, where he continues to fight crime.

WARBIRD

CAROL DANVERS had intended to have a career in the U.S. Air Force; however she was assigned to military intelligence and became a top agent. She grew disillusioned with the world of espionage, resigned her commission and became the head of security at a N.A.S.A. space center. There she first met the Kree warrior known as Captain Mar-Vell. While Mar-Vell fought a Kree rival, Danvers was accidentally irradiated by unknown energies. She became an adventurer calling herself Ms. Marvel.

WELL, I GUESS I'M A FULL-FLEDGED AVENGER NOW! DOES IT SHOW?

YOU MEAN, ASIDE FROM THAT TELL-TALE GLOW OF PRIDE?

CONGRATULATIONS, MS. M. IT'LL BE A PLEASURE AVENGING WITH YOU!

PROUD TO JOIN
After helping the Avengers battle Michael Korvac, Ms. Marvel was admitted to the team when the Scarlet Witch requested an extended leave of absence.

ENTER MS. MARVEL
The radiation had changed Carol's genetic structure, making her part-Kree. She discovered that she also possessed superhuman strength, the ability to fly and a clairvoyant "seventh sense." After adopting the costumed identity of Ms. Marvel, Danvers moved to New York City where she worked as a magazine editor and freelance writer.

Warbird fires psionic energy from her hands.

BINARY
While battling the mutant Rogue, Ms. Marvel lost her superpowers. An alien race exposed her to a ray that triggered her Kree genes and enabled her to emit electromagnetic energy. Carol took the name Binary, but when her original powers returned, she changed her name to Warbird.

BLAST IT, WANDA. THERE ISN'T A FATHER!

PLEASE, MS. MARVEL, JUST TRY TO STAY CALM.

...MOTHER.

The Marcus Mystery
While Ms. Marvel, Danvers fell under the spell of a ghostly being named Marcus who desired a physical body. She became pregnant, and in only a few days, gave birth to Marcus himself! He tried to convince her to live in limbo with him.

TWO-GUN KID

BORN IN THE EAST OF THE USA, Matthew Hawk studied law and moved to the western frontier town of Tombstone, Arizona shortly after the American Civil War. He soon fell foul of bullies; however, a retired gunfighter taught him how to use a six-gun with deadly accuracy. Matt developed a lightning-fast draw and, adopting the moniker the Two-Gun Kid, wore a mask to conceal his identity from trigger-happy gunslingers.

When Matt Hawk couldn't protect the innocent, the masked Two-Gun Kid rode to their defense mounted on Thunder.

WAY OUT WEST

Moondragon, Thor and Hawkeye of the Avengers once journeyed back in time to the Old West to battle Kang the Conqueror. Teaming up with the Two-Gun Kid, the Avengers fought a monster mutated from a coyote and defeated Kang. Afterwards, the Kid decided to visit the future and accompanied the Avengers when they returned to the 20th century.

Thunder was the fastest and smartest horse in Tombstone.

The Two-Gun Kid and his partners Moondragon, Hawkeye and Thor defy Kang's threats to destroy every Avenger who has ever lived.

Back from the Future

On leave from the Avengers, Hawkeye decided to tour the American southwest with the Two-Gun Kid. Their adventuring was cut short when the Two-Gun Kid was snatched by the Collector, who was attempting to gather a full set of Avengers. After he was rescued, Two-Gun used the Collector's technology to return to Tombstone and fight crime.

When Legends Live

With the aid of the Avengers, Red Wolf managed to save his people from ruthless developers who had planned to drive them off the reservation. Following the legend of previous Red Wolves, Talltrees adopted a wolf cub, he named Lobo. They trained together until they almost thought as one. Red Wolf later joined the Rangers, a team of superhumans based in the American Southwest.

RED WOLF

WILL TALLTREES was a Native American who grew up on the Cheyenne Reservation in Wolf Point, Montana. His parents often told him the legend of Red Wolf, a superhuman champion who protected the Cheyenne. When his family was murdered by greedy businessmen, Talltrees begged the gods for the power to avenge them. Owayodata, the Wolf-Spirit heard his prayers and transformed him into a modern day Red Wolf.

Man on a Mission

A former soldier and an expert fighter, Talltrees had gained superhuman strength by dancing the Dance of the Red Wolf. He was so intent on gaining justice for his people that he found it hard to accept help—even from Earth's mightiest!

Red Wolf's tracking skills surprised the Avengers.

WHIZZER

BITTEN BY A POISONOUS SNAKE, Robert Frank was injected with a serum that contained mongoose blood. The serum triggered Frank's latent mutant abilities and gave him superhuman speed. Calling himself the Whizzer, Frank was a costumed hero during the 1940s and joined the All-Winners Squad alongside Captain America, Sub-Mariner, and the Human Torch. He later married Madeline Joyce, also known as the heroine Miss America.

NUKLO

Long after he retired, the Whizzer begged the Avengers to protect his son who had been imprisoned in a Chrono-Module because he had become a walking nuclear reactor.

MISTAKEN BELIEF

For a brief time, Frank believed that Quicksilver and the Scarlet Witch were his children. He suffered a fatal heart attack before learning the truth.

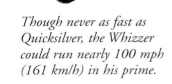

Though never as fast as Quicksilver, the Whizzer could run nearly 100 mph (161 km/h) in his prime.

"THE THREAT CROSS-COUNTRY IS AS NOTHING COMPARED TO WHAT MY KREE-BORN SENSES, MERE MINUTES AGO, DETECTED NEAR *HERE!*"

YEAH-- *ABOUT* THAT: I DON'T MIND RUNNIN' MY *FEET* OFF --

-- IF I *KNOW* WHAT I'M RUNNIN' *AFTER!*

CAPTAIN MAR-VELL

MAR-VELL WAS AN ALIEN sent to spy on the Earth, but he ended up sacrificing his life to defend it. A captain in the space fleet of the militaristic Kree Empire, Mar-Vell was sent to observe the planet's space programs. In time, Mar-Vell came to admire the people of Earth. Instead of sabotaging their efforts to reach the stars, Mar-Vell secretly aided them.

MARVEL'S SPACE-BORN SUPER-HERO!
CAPTAIN MARVEL
MARVEL COMICS GROUP 12¢ 1 MAY
BIG PREMIERE ISSUE!
"OUT OF THE HOLOCAUST... A HERO!"

WAR HERO
Mar-Vell had fought bravely in several battles with the Skrulls, shape-changing aliens who were the Kree's hereditary enemies.

BONDED

Returning to Earth after a space mission, Mar-Vell was hurled into the Negative Zone, an antimatter universe in another dimension. He remained trapped until he made telepathic contact with Rick Jones, once of the Teen Brigade. Mar-Vell led Rick to an abandoned Kree base on Earth, where Rick found a pair of "nega-bands." Placed together, the bands allowed Mar-Vell and Rick to switch places so Mar-Vell could escape the Negative Zone for brief periods.

Mar-Vell's nega-bands gave him superhuman strength and the ability to fly.

--BUT *RONAN* NO LONGER CARES WHAT IT *IS.*

WITH THESE *OTHERS* IN MY GRASP, WHAT CAN A MERE *SPEED-STER* AND AN UNTRIED *YOUTH* HOPE TO ACHIEVE?

MY CALCULATIONS, MASTER, ARE: *NOTHING.*

Galactic Threat
Mar-Vell turned to the Avengers when he learned that Ronan the Accuser planned to seize the Kree empire and declare war on the Skrulls. Ronan's victory was assured, until the Supreme Intelligence gave Rick Jones the power to save the universe.

YOU WERE RIGHT. ISSAC CONFIRMS THE FINDINGS OF YOUR COSMIC SENSES.

I'M SORRY...

I WAS SURE MY SENSES WERE RIGHT. I DETECTED THE DISEASE A COUPLE OF WEEKS AGO.

Protector of the Universe
After the Kree/Skrull War, Mar-Vell met a being named Eon who served as a cosmic caretaker. Eon gave him a psionic ability called "cosmic awareness" that allowed Mar-Vell to sense threats to the galaxy and appointed him "Protector of the Universe." But then Mar-Vell discovered he was dying of cancer.

GENIS-VELL
After Mar-Vell's death, his son Genis-Vell donned the nega-bands and became bonded with Rick Jones. Like his dad, Genis-Vell is super-strong, can fly through space and fire force bolts from his bands.

SUPREME INTELLIGENCE

RULER OF THE KREE EMPIRE for untold centuries, the Supreme Intelligence is a vast cybernetic/organic computer system. Incorporating the brain patterns of the greatest Kree statesmen, philosophers and scientists, the Intelligence is based on Kree-La, prime planet of the Kree Empire and directs all aspects of Kree society. The Intelligence's chief fear is that the Kree race may have reached an evolutionary dead end.

PSIONIC POWER
Thanks to the Intelligence, Rick was able to mentally freeze the Skrull armada and the Kree forces, ending the Kree/Skrull war.

THE EXPERIMENT
Believing mankind had the ability to keep evolving, the Intelligence decided to combine the genetic structure of a human, Rick Jones, and a Kree warrior, Captain Mar-Vell. The Intelligence hurled Mar-Vell into the Negative Zone and enabled him to contact Rick. When the evil Ronan tried to take over the empire and start a war, the Intelligence decided to activate Jones' psionic powers.

YOU ARE IN THE PRESENCE OF THE *INTELLIGENCE SUPREME*...RIGHTFUL *RULER* OF THE ETERNAL KREE, UNTIL I WAS OVERTHROWN BY THE USURPER WITHOUT.

NO, YOUTH...I AM *NOT* A TRULY LIVING CREATURE, BUT THE SUM AND SUBSTANCE OF THE *MIGHTIEST MINDS* OF UNTOLD MILLENNIA OF KREE HISTORY---

A *MULTIPLICITY* OF GENIUSES, MADE MANIFEST IN *ONE* BEING, *ONE* ENTITY.

FAAANTASTIC! I'VE SEEN UGLY BEFORE-- BUT MAN, YOU'RE UGLY!

SUPREME FAILURE
The Intelligence wished to add Rick and Mar-Vell to its brain bank, but failed when it discovered that mankind could not be used to jumpstart the Kree's evolution.

FSSSMMM

--I DON'T THINK SO AT *ALL!*

I DON'T THINK SO LITTLE MAN--

...MY OWN SUPERAVOR...

...KOEATH THE PROWLER...

WHA--?! WHAT'S HAPPENING?!

Operation: Galactic Storm
Desperate to revitalize the Kree, the Intelligence started a war between the Kree and the Shi'ar. It exploded a "nega-bomb" that slaughtered most of the Kree, but rekindled the evolutionary process in the survivors. Outraged, many of the Avengers wanted to destroy the Intelligence, but its consciousness could not be killed.

Starforce
Though the Intelligence can communicate through the use of a giant holographic computer screen, it cannot move. Whenever it needs a specific job done, it employs Starforce—its very own team of superhuman Kree warriors, who are highly skilled in all forms of combat.

> JUST AS OUR *FOES* FIND STRENGTH IN *UNION*, SO SHALL *WE*.

LEGION of the UNLIVING

> THE LEGION OF THE UNLIVING!

THERE'S NO REST for the wicked... Not even when you're dead. Determined to find the Celestial Madonna and thereby become the most powerful man in the universe, Kang attacked the Avengers. Working with Immortus, one of his alternate identities, Kang gathering a gruesome band who were all currently dead. In the dungeons of Immortus' castle, Kang pitted his undead band against the Avengers.

THE FIRST LEGION

The first Legion consisted of the Frankenstein Monster, Wonder Man, the Human Torch, Baron Zemo, the ghost of the Flying Dutchman and the assassin Midnight. After forcing Kang to flee for his life, the Avengers managed to send them all back to their respective time periods.

THE SECOND LEGION

The Second Legion

The Grandmaster formed a new Legion that included former Avengers friends like the Swordsman, Captain Mar-Vell, Drax the Destroyer and Bucky and old enemies like the Executioner, Nighthawk, Hyperion, the Red Guardian, the Black Knight, Baron Blood, Michael Korvac, Death Adder, Dracula, Terrax, and the original Green Goblin.

The Third Legion

Immortus formed a legion to capture Scarlet Witch with the Black Knight, Grim Reaper, an Iron Man double, Swordsman, Toro, Left-Winger, Right-Winger, and Oort the Living Comet.

The Grim Reaper is now a vengeful spirit.

> TOO LONG HAVE YOU KILLED -- *CALLOUSLY, CRUELLY!* TOO LONG! IT'S TIME FOR YOUR PAST TO *CATCH UP* TO YOU --

> -- FOR YOU TO PAY THE *PRICE!*

The Fourth Legion

Claiming that the Avengers were all murderers, the Grim Reaper suddenly appeared and summoned a fourth legion that included Captain Mar-Vell, Doctor Druid, Hellcat, Mockingbird, Swordsman, Thunderstrike and Wonder Man.

The LETHAL LEGION

HAVING SWORN to punish the Avengers for allowing his brother Wonder Man to die, the Grim Reaper assembled a team of superhuman criminals he called his Lethal Legion. The original members were Living Laser, Man-Ape, Swordsman and Erik Josten, alias Power Man. The Reaper's first victim was the Black Panther. He then dispatched other Legion members to various locations to divide and conquer the other Avengers.

Hourglass of Doom

The Reaper placed his Avengers captives in a giant hourglass filled with a deadly gas. Power Man went after the Vision, the last Avenger, but was defeated. Once the Vision freed his teammates, they quickly defeated the Lethal Legion.

A SECOND LEGION

Claiming that he had the means to enhance their powers, Count Nefaria formed a new Lethal Legion. It consisted of Living Laser, Whirlwind (a mutant who could rotate his body at super-speed) and Erik Josten who had become the new Goliath. The Count later betrayed his new Legion by stealing all their powers.

A Third and Fourth Legion

The Grim Reaper returned with a third version of the Legion. He attacked the West Coast Avengers with a team comprising the Black Talon, Goliath, Man-Ape, Nekra and Ultron. Satannish, a demon from an alternate dimension formed a *fourth* Legion by resurrecting dead criminals and giving them superhuman powers.

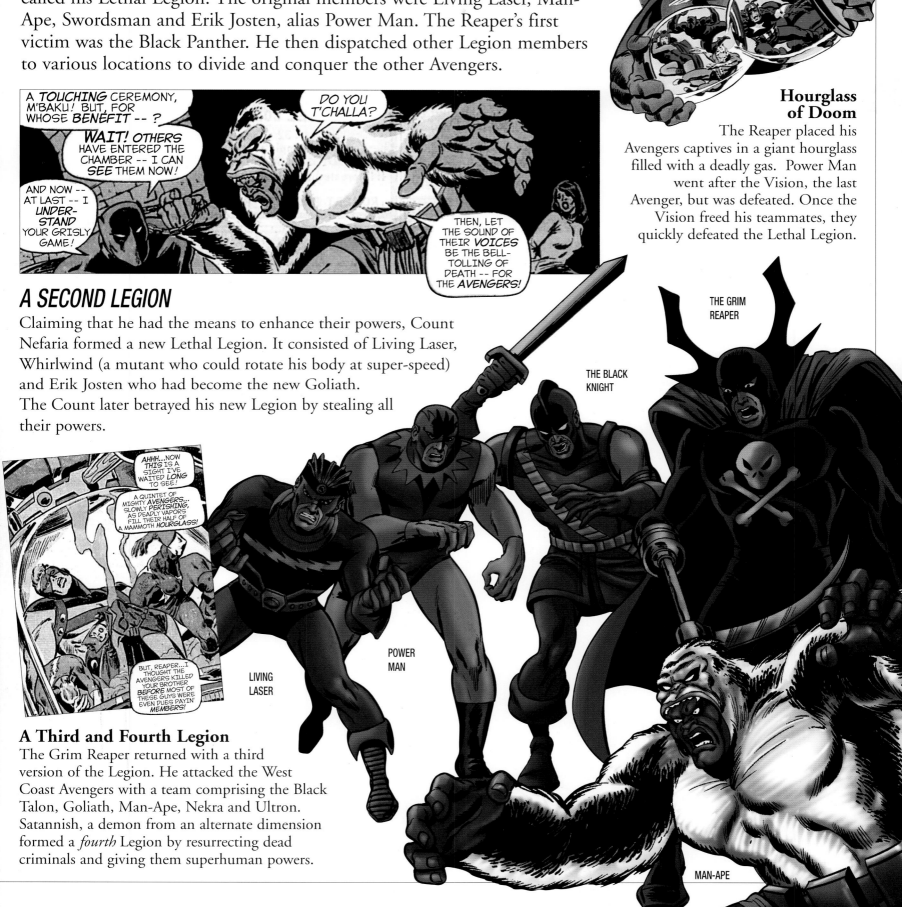

THE GRIM REAPER

THE BLACK KNIGHT

POWER MAN

LIVING LASER

MAN-APE

GUARDIANS of the GALAXY

The Guardians are the Avengers of the 31st century.

IN A POSSIBLE FUTURE, an alien race called the Badoon invaded our solar system in the 31st century and a team of adventurers banded together to oppose them. The Guardians were made up of the mysterious Starhawk, the super-strong Charlie-27, the silicon-based Marinex, the agile Nikki, Yondu the archer and Vance Astro, an American astronaut awakened after ages in suspended animation.

The Korvac Saga

Cyborg Michael Korvac was a computer genius who worked for the Badoon. He gained vast power from an alien ship and traveled back in time to reshape the universe. The Guardians joined with the Avengers to stop him.

Many Avengers were severely injured during the battle, but Korvac was eventually defeated.

HENRY GYRICH

HENRY PETER GYRICH does everything by the book. An agent for the National Security Council, he was assigned to investigate reports of "irregularities" concerning the Avengers. He entered the Mansion through a gaping hole in the side of the building, caused by a recent battle with Count Nefaria.

The Bean-Counter

Threatening to cancel the Avengers' special privileges—access to classified intelligence and exemption from air-traffic controls—Gyrich instituted stringent new policies on security. He also decided who was and who wasn't qualified to join the team's new roster.

Falcon was not pleased to learn that he was asked to join the Avengers because Gyrich had insisted that the team provide equal opportunities for minorities.

S.H.I.E.L.D.

The S.H.I.E.L.D. Helicarrier is a huge airborne command base.

THE SUPREME Headquarters International Espionage Law-enforcement Division is a worldwide intelligence and peace-keeping force that answers to the United Nations Security Council. It is dedicated to protecting the nations of Earth from global and extraterrestrial threats and has offices in many of the world's major cities.

Agent Programs

S.H.I.E.L.D. exchanges intelligence with the Fantastic Four and the Avengers. It has tried to enlist Captain America and Black Widow as full-time agents and has sent them on many freelance assignments. S.H.I.E.L.D. has also instituted programs to train super-agents, such as Quasar.

*WEAPON SYSTEMS
Some of S.H.I.E.L.D.'s greatest assets are its advanced weaponry and sophisticated technology, most of which was designed by Tony Stark and built by Stark Industries.*

WE KNOW CRADPOCK -- EVEN IF YOU DON'T.

THIS IS WHAT HAPPENED, INFLUENCE-PEDDLER! IRON MAN IS WHAT HAPPENED!!!

BARELY STRENGTH ENOUGH-- TO REMOVE MY POWER-POPS-- AND DIRECT ALL THE ELECTRICAL ENERGY THEY STORE--AT THE MANDROIDS.

BUT, SINCE I DESIGNED THOSE THINGS--AS TONY STARK--

--I KNOW THAT OUGHT TO BE-- PLENTY!

Shifting Agendas

Although the Avengers and S.H.I.E.L.D. often work together, they have also come into conflict on occasion. When the Kree/Skrull War started to heat up, the U.S. government appointed an Alien Activities Commission that ordered S.H.I.E.L.D. to arrest the Avengers for harboring extraterrestrials. However, S.H.I.E.L.D. later made amends by lending the team a spacecraft.

THE MANDROIDS

S.H.I.E.L.D.'s Mandroid armor is for use against superhuman opponents. The suit gives superhuman strength and is equipped with stun cannons, lasers, and a tractor beam that can freeze or repel.

Nick Fury

The director of S.H.I.E.L.D. is a former solder who once led a squad called the Howling Commandos. He rose to the rank of Colonel before leaving the military to become a C.I.A. agent. He accepted the directorship with the understanding that he would have authority over all field missions. Fury is gruff and decisive, but his personal integrity has seen S.H.I.E.L.D. through many crises.

A serum called the Infinity Formula helps keep Fury in prime physical shape.

NICK FURY, AGENT OF... S.H.I.E.L.D.

MARVEL COMICS GROUP 12¢ 4 SEP

SHIELD ORIGIN ISSUE

Fury has trained as a paratrooper, demolition expert, and Army Ranger.

THE AVENGERS IN THE 1980s

WHEN THE 1980s BEGAN, Iron Man was chairman and the Avengers were made up of Ms. Marvel, Captain America, Scarlet Witch, Vision, Wasp, Beast and Falcon. Scripter David Michelinie and penciler John Byrne started the new decade with a battle with the Grey Gargoyle, one of Thor's old villains. Roger Stern and Al Milgrom took over the creative chores in 1983 as the new Captain Marvel joined the team and Hank Pym left.

After a successful four-issue tryout, the West Coast Avengers were awarded their own title in 1985 which was written by Steve Englehart and drawn by Al Milgrom. John Buscema returned to pencil the regular Avengers title and the team took a trip the Savage Land.

As the decade progressed, we learned that there was more than one Kang running around the multiverse, and the new Baron Zemo invaded the Avengers' Mansion. A third Avengers title was launched in 1987, initially called Solo Avengers, but later renamed Avengers Spotlight. It featured a lead Hawkeye story followed by solo stories of the various Avengers. The team were involved in Inferno, a major crossover that ran across the entire line of Marvel titles in 1988, and they followed this adventure with Evolutionary War. As the decade drew to a close, John Byrne took over the art and writing of the West Coast book and was joined on the East Coast title by penciler Paul Ryan.

The Avengers #200 (Oct. 1980) Temporal anomalies plague New York as Ms. Marvel gives birth to a son who reaches adulthood within mere hours. *(Cover by George Perez and Terry Austin).*

The Avengers #213 (Nov. 1981) Captain America charges Yellowjacket recklessness. *(Cover by Bob Hall and Dan Green)*

1980

The Avengers #192 (Feb. 1980) Iron Man and Wonder Man visit the Steel City. *(Cover by George Perez and Joe Sinnott)*

1981

The Avengers Annual #10 (1981) Rogue absorbs Ms. Marvel's superhuman powers. *(Cover by Al Milgrom)*

1982

The Avengers #223 (Sept. 1982) Hawkeye and Ant-Man battle the Taskmaster. *(Cover by Ed Hannigan and Klaus Janson)*

1984

The Avengers #243 (May 1984) The Vision is linked with an alien super-computer. *(Cover by Al Milgrom and Joe Sinnott)*

The Avengers #300 (Feb. 1989) The Avengers celebrate 300 hundred issues with the introduction of a new team. *(Cover by John Buscema and Tom Palmer)*

The Avengers #273 (Nov. 1986)
The Marvel Universe celebrates its 35th Anniversary with a series of dramatic portrait covers. *(Cover by John Buscema and Tom Palmer)*

1985

The Avengers #255 (May 1985) Captain Marvel is kidnapped by space pirates. *(Painting by Tom Palmer)*

1987

The Avengers #277 (March 1987) Captain America faces a new Baron Zemo. *(Cover by John Buscema and Tom Palmer)*

1988

The Avengers #288 (Feb. 1988) The Sentry attacks the team. *(Cover by John Buscema and Tom Palmer)*

1989

The Avengers #302 (April 1989) East and West Coast team against the Super-Nova. *(Cover by John Buscema and Tom Palmer)*

U.S. AGENT

*J*OHN WALKER longed to honor the memory of his elder brother, a helicopter pilot who died in the Vietnam War, by becoming a military hero. After a spell in the army, John contacted the mysterious Power Broker, who had designed a process that gave people superhuman strength. John became the Super-Patriot, a costumed hero who claimed to stand for American ideals of freedom and justice.

HEADING
The U.S. Agent always believed that Captain America was too lenient on criminals and out of touch with contemporary American values.

CLASH OF THE CAPTAINS
The government granted Walker the name U.S. Agent, but that was not prestigious enough for him. He tried to wrest the mantle of Captain America from Steve Rogers, whom called a traitor to his country.

Moonknight's ghostlike presence strikes fear into his enemies.

MOONKNIGHT

*M*ARC SPECTOR was always a man of mystery. A former heavyweight boxer, Marine and C.I.A. agent, he was working as a mercenary when he was attacked and left for dead near an archeological dig in Egypt. He came around close to the statue of Khonshu, Egyptian god of the moon. Believing he had been spared for a reason, Spector became the moon's knight of vengeance.

WHITE KNIGHT
Spector made a costume from the white cloth wrapped around the statue.

Under Orders
Spector used his vast fortune to fight crime for many years. The spirit of Khonshu then ordered him to join the West Coast Avengers. Spector complied and helped the team battle the criminal cartel known as the Zodiac. Khonshu later compelled Spector to resign from the team.

HUMAN TORCH

FLAMING MENACE
The news media proclaimed the Torch a monster when it first appeared in public.

*T*HE FIRST HERO known as the Human Torch was born from failure. Professor Phineas T. Horton was a pioneer in the field of artificial intelligence and built one of the world's first androids in 1939. Unfortunately, it burst into flame when exposed to oxygen. In time, however, the android learned to control its flame, took the name Jim Hammond, and became a crime-fighter.

EARLY ALLIES

The Torch adopted a young mutant named Toro who had similar powers. When World War II erupted, the Torch and Toro joined with the Sub-Mariner, Captain America and Bucky to form the Invaders and fight the Nazis. After the war, they founded the All-Winners Squad.

LORD OF FIRE

The Human Torch could cover his whole body with flame and control every flame in his immediate vicinity. He could also fly, form flaming constructs, fire bursts of flame, and absorb heat from outside sources.

A New Life

After he retired, Hammond was reprogrammed by the criminal Mad Thinker and sent to attack Johnny Storm, the present-day Torch. Hammond later returned to crime-fighting with the West Coast Avengers and the reformed Invaders.

West Coast Avengers

To strengthen the Avengers' ability to protect the Earth, the Vision sent Hawkeye to Los Angeles to form a West Coast branch. The shifting membership would include Hawkeye, Mockingbird, Tigra, Wonder Man, Hank Pym, the Wasp, the Thing, War Machine, the Bill Foster version of Goliath, Quicksilver, the Scarlet Witch and the Vision. The team battled super-enemies like Graviton, the master of gravity, the Grim Reaper's Lethal Legion, Ultron and Magneto. The team disbanded after its base was destroyed.

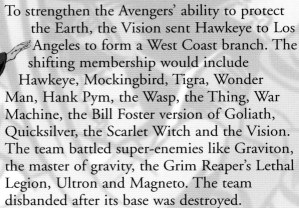

FIREBIRD

BONITA JUAREZ was sure she had been singled out for greatness. A young American Indian living with her grandmother, Bonita was walking in the desert one night near Albuquerque, New Mexico, when a huge ball of cold fire crashed down from the sky, bathing her in unknown radiations. She soon discovered that she could fly and project blasts of heat from her body in the rough shape of a bird.

INSPIRED

Bonita believed the fireball was a gift from the firebird, a legendary creature of Native American myth. She fashioned a costume and began using her powers to fight crime and to help people. Although Bonita later learned that her powers were the result of waste products generated by an alien race's experiments, she didn't lose confidence in her heroic role as Firebird.

The Rangers

In a situation that echoed the Avengers' origin, Firebird intercepted a distress call about the Hulk on a rampage in the Southwestern U.S.A. When she arrived there, she met other crime-fighters—Red Wolf, Texas Twister, Shooting Star, and the Night Rider. Calling themselves the Rangers, the heroes banded together to protect the region.

LA ESPIRITA
While calling herself La Espirita, Bonita grew close to Hank Pym.

West Coast Comrades

Firebird first met the West Coast Avengers when she traveled to Los Angeles to battle Master Pandemonium, an ex-movie actor who had turned to sorcery. She traveled with the Avengers to the dimension of the Cat People, fought alongside the team against a demonic Shooting Star, and helped rescue the Avengers when they were trapped in the past. However, Firebird never became a member.

PANDEMONIUM REIGNS
Master Pandemonium's body was a gateway for demonic forces. Firebird blasted him with a fireball to no avail.

GREAT LAKES AVENGERS

BIG BERTHA
Bertha can absorb bullets fired at her by a machine-gun toting into her considerable body—and fire them right back at him!

CRAIG HOLLIS couldn't die. He played with alligators, held exploding sticks of dynamite, drank toxic chemicals—but never came to harm. It finally dawned on him that he was blest with a super-power and he decided to become Mr. Immortal, a crime-fighter. His ability couldn't stop criminals, so he advertised for help; some decidedly unusual individuals replied.

THE ROLL CALL

The linup of Mr. Immortal's Great Lakes Avengers team would comprise: Doorman, a living portal; Ashley Crawford, alias Big Bertha, a supermodel who could increase her size and strength to superhuman levels; Dr. Ventura, alias Flatman, who could make his body wafer thin; the alien named Dinah Shore, who could fly and generate blasts of sonic energy; and, later, Squirrel Girl, who could communicate with squirrels.

Team work
The GLA assisted the West Coasters against an alien virus which called itself "That Which Endures" and claimed to control the evolutionary process of all life on Earth. They were later tricked into attacking Captain America in a failed attempt to steal his indestructible shield.

OKAY, FLATMAN...
READY WHEN YOU ARE!
...GO!
READY AS I'LL EVER BE, D.M. HERE I...

Dinah's Magic Words
Although an arrogant hothead, Mr. Immortal truly loved Dinah Shore, a member of an ancient and unknown race with razor-sharp wings. Craig was the only one on the team who understood her alien tongue. Faced with the prospect of dealing with the press, who were clamoring for information about the new team, he had a sudden, violent attack of nerves. Fortunately, the unearthly Dinah Shore managed to calm him down with a few, well-chosen "hypersonic" words.

CALM DOWN! CALM DOWN!
BIG BERTHA! I CAN'T GET HIM TO SIMMER DOWN!
TAKE IT EASY, FLATMAN.
DINAH... LOOKS LIKE WE NEED YOUR MAGIC TOUCH HERE...

*^^^*
WORKS EVERY TIME! I SURE WISH WE KNEW WHAT IT IS SHE DOES!
SOME KIND OF HYPERSONIC, I GUESS. I DON'T KNOW THAT IT MATTERS, AS LONG AS IT CALMS HIM.

NEW RECRUIT Dinah Shore was killed by Maelstrom, who could control kinetic energy. Her replacement, Doug Taggert, had a costume that mimicked a grasshopper's powers, but did not survive long.

TIGRA

GREER GRANT NELSON was a lab assistant working for Dr. Joanne Rumulo when she took part in an experiment to enhance her physical abilities. She gained superhuman strength, speed, and agility and became a costumed crime-fighter called the Cat. Exposed to a lethal dose of radiation, Greer learned she was a member of the Cat People, a race that had magically evolved from cats.

WERE-TIGER

To save Greer's life, Dr. Rumulo magically transformed Greer into a new version of the Cat People's most sacred warrior—Tigra, a were-creature with superhuman abilities. Greer resumed her crime-fighting career, occasionally teaming-up with Red Wolf, Spider-Man, and the Fantastic Four. The influence of Moondragon led Tigra to seek Avengers membership.

Tigra Meets Molecule Man

Tigra never enjoyed being an Avenger. Though she proved herself in battle, she never quite believed that she fit in with the other members. When the Molecule Man, a powerful super-villain who could control matter, defeated the Avengers, Tigra convinced him to see a therapist and to stop trying to conquer the Earth. She also decided to quit being an Avenger.

CONFLICTED CAT
Tigra slowly began to lose control of her catlike nature. She returned to the Cat People who helped her to regain the human side of her personality.

Feline Force

Tigra possesses superhuman strength, speed and reflexes and amazingly acute senses of smell, hearing, and vision. She is able to follow any trail and can see in the dark. As agile as a cat, she is a skilled gymnast who can perform complex maneuvers with ease. Her catlike tendencies don't end there, however: she also has a domestic cat's need for affection and security.

Going Solo

After working as a private detective, Tigra accepted Hawkeye's invitation to join the West Coast Avengers, helping them against super-villains like Whirlwind, the human top. She now works as a solo crime-fighter.

SHE-HULK

JENNIFER WALTERS' widowed father was a Los Angeles County Sheriff and he often sent his rebellious daughter to visit her mother's relatives, the Banners. Jennifer admired her older cousin Bruce and they spent a lot of time together. While Bruce studied nuclear physics and became the Hulk, Jennifer went to law school and, to her father's annoyance, became a defense attorney.

UNEXPECTED SIDE-EFFECTS
Banner didn't realize how Jennifer's body would react to his mutated blood.

GIRL POWER

Some time after the exposure to gamma rays that turned him into the Hulk, Bruce was visiting Jennifer when she was attacked by criminals. Bruce knew that he and Jennifer had the same blood type and saved her life with an emergency transfusion. However, his gamma-irradiated blood gave Jennifer the power to transform into a female version of the Hulk, 6ft 7in (2 meters) tall.

Call me She Hulk

Bruce Banner and the Hulk usually had two different personalities, but She-Hulk retained Jennifer's mind and disposition. She wasn't quite as strong as her cousin, but could still lift nearly 75 tons! Jennifer moved to New York City and won an invitation from the Wasp to join the Avengers after helping to defeat Fabian Stankowicz, the Mechano-Marauder. The She-Hulk later battled Egghead, Whirlwind and Taskmaster. Apart from a brief spell with the Fantastic Four, she has stayed with the Avengers.

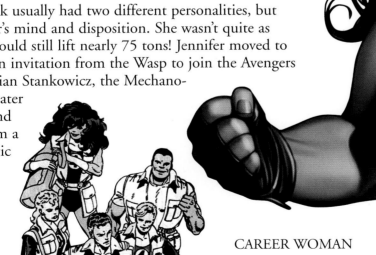

Single Green Female

Jennifer lost the ability to change back to her normal human form after being exposed to a burst of gamma rays— and that was fine by her because she loved being the She-Hulk.

CAREER WOMAN
Jennifer continues to practice law as She-Hulk, often representing other heroes. However, she would rather fight bad guys.

PHOTON

MONICA RAMBEAU loved the sea and dreamed of captaining her own ship. She joined the New Orleans Harbor Patrol and rose to the rank of lieutenant. Trying to destroy an energy-disruptor weapon developed by a South American terrorist, Monica was exposed to energies from another dimension and turned into living energy.

IN A FLASH, THE BLACK-AND-SILVER-CLAD WOMAN TRANSFORMS INTO A BOLT OF PURE ELECTRICAL ENERGY!

Big Bangs
Monica can transform her body into energy, enabling flight, and direct powerful blasts through her hands.

Monica first called herself Captain Marvel, but changed her name to Photon.

A HARD WORKER

Anxious to learn how to control her powers, Monica sought help from the Avengers. Calling herself Captain Marvel, she joined the team and received training in unarmed combat from Captain America himself. She proved herself such a valuable member of the team that she was elected chairman of the Avengers.

THAT SOUNDED SUITABLY MYSTERIOUS.

I WONDER WHAT'S UP. PERHAPS THE SUB-MARINER'S RETURNED. WELL, I'LL SOON FIND OUT!

The Hand of the Infinites

After quitting the Harbor Patrol, Monica worked as a charter-boat captain in New Orleans. Since she could travel at the speed of light, commuting to Avengers Mansion was not a problem for her. Photon joined the team to battle against a gargantuan alien race called the Infinites, who intended to steal the entire Milky Way galaxy. Photon merged her consciousness with the other Avengers and helped drive the creatures away.

Photon can make herself invisible and create holographic images.

I AM CALLED PHOTON! YOU MUST UNDERSTAND—LIFE, IN ALL ITS MANY FORMS IS SO VERY PRECIOUS...

POWER LOSS
When the Sub-Mariner's wife Marrina turned into a reptilian monster, Photon tried to use electrical energy to stun the creature. She touched water, and the electric shock caused Photon to lose most of her energy. It took her months to regain her powers.

HER EYES! THEY STILL SPARK!

CAPTAIN MARVEL YET LIVES. BUT SHE IS IN THE FINAL STAGES OF EXHAUSTION.

SHE-HULK, ALERT NEW YORK HOSPITAL! TELL THE EMERGENCY ROOM TO EXPECT ME MOMENTARILY!

WAIT A MOMENT -- MY QUANTUM-BANDS ARE STARTING TO GLOW --

QUASAR

ARMY VETERAN Wendell Vaughn was planning to become a S.H.I.E.L.D. agent when fate took a hand. Reed Richards had recently confiscated a pair of alien energy-manipulating bands. S.H.I.E.L.D. hired Wendell's dad to study them. Dr. Vaughn tested them on his son and Wendell was horrified to discover that the bands bonded themselves to his wrists as soon as he donned them. He was immediately given the code name "Marvel Man" and drafted into S.H.I.E.L.D.S.'s super-agent program.

I'M GOING OUT TO INVESTIGATE SOMETHING! I'LL BE BACK AS SOON AS I CAN!

ALIEN CALL
Eon is a cosmic custodian, who appoints agents to protect the universe. After the death of Captain Mar-Vell, the alien chose Quasar as his successor and made contact with him by means of a dimensional portal.

Quasar's quantum bands are composed of unknown materials.

GALACTIC WAR

Wendell changed his name to Quasar and joined the Avengers after helping them defeat Super-Nova, a giant alien. He was also present when the Lava Men launched an attack on Avengers Island and when the team became involved in a war between the Kree and Shi'ar races, which became known as *Operation: Galactic Storm.*

LAVA MEN... ??

SOME OF THE **FIRST** FOES THE AVENGERS **DID** FACE!

FOLLOW ME!

SOMEONE OUGHT TO REMIND THE GOLDEN BOY SCOUT WITH THE COSMIC ACCESSORIES THAT WE **HAPPEN** TO BE A TEAM!

AND SOMEBODY OUGHTA REMIND **YOU** THAT YOU'RE NOT GOD'S GIFT TO SUPER HEROES, LADY! SHEEESH!

LIGHT SPEED
Quasar flies by surrounding himself with an energy field and moving at light speed. He can also create small holes in space that allow him to jump from one galaxy to another.

Quantum Energy
Quasar believes that his wristbands draw energy from a place called the Quantum Zone. The bands enable him to manipulate electromagnetic force in a variety of ways. He can create solid objects out of pure energy, forming them into any shape that he can imagine such as spheres, cones, cubes, hammers, or cages. He can also siphon energy from virtually any power source and can project beams of concussive force. While he has no control over psionic energy, he has programmed the quantum-bands to protect his mind from telepathic attacks.

Quasar left the Avengers to devote more time to protecting the universe.

DOCTOR DRUID

ANTONY DRUID was a psychiatrist who received his medical degree from Harvard University. After practicing for several years, he retired to study the occult, becoming an authority on Celtic lore and the author of several books on magic. He was then summoned to Tibet, where an Asian mystic activated his latent supernatural abilities.

I'VE HAD A STRANGE UNPLEASANT *BUZZING* IN MY HEAD THE PAST HALF-HOUR, AND I CAN'T SHAKE THE FEELING THAT THE *AVENGERS* ARE IN SOME WAY CONNECTED--

MASS HYPNOSIS
Druid can mesmerize an individual or a crowd. His hypnotic powers enable him to create any illusion he wishes.

FOR SUDDENLY...

AVENGERS--HEAR ME! YOU HAVE BEEN CHOSEN--FOR A MOST URGENT AND PERILOUS MISSION!

HEY! YOU CAN'T JUST WALK IN HERE!

EVIDENTLY HE CAN, WHOEVER HE IS-- THOUGH I'D LIKE TO LEARN HOW!

DOCTOR'S ORDERS

By magical means, Druid learned that the spirit of Dane Whitman, the Black Knight, was trapped in the 12th century and that the Fomor, a race of extra-dimensional beings, planned to conquer Earth. Instead of asking for help, Druid stormed into Avengers Mansion, hypnotized the team and sent them into the past to rescue the Knight and save the planet.

Patent Remedy

The Avengers were annoyed with Druid's arrogance and they parted on bad terms. But the team had cause to thank the Doctor when he used his hypnotic powers to defeat Baron Zemo and his Masters of Evil, who had invaded the Avengers Mansion. The Avengers rewarded him with an invitation to join the team.

YOU ?! BUT THE NEEDLER SHOULD HAVE KEPT YOU PARALYZED FOR *HOURS!*

YOU MUST BE RESPONSIBLE FOR THIS! SOMEHOW YOU FORCED BLACKOUT TO *DEFY* ME!

NO, I MERELY UNSHACKLED HIS MIND...

Influence of Evil

Druid and the Avengers fell out when, influenced by Ravonna the Terminatrix, he used his powers to manipulate the team. When the Avengers freed themselves, Druid and Ravonna fled. Druid later broke with Ravonna, apologized to the Avengers, and devoted himself to fighting supernatural menaces.

CELTIC LORE
Thanks to his study of Celtic magic, Druid can create many magical feats through the use of special candles, potions, symbols, chants and runes.

MENTAL CONTROL
Druid can project his thoughts into another's mind to influence the way a person thinks and behaves.

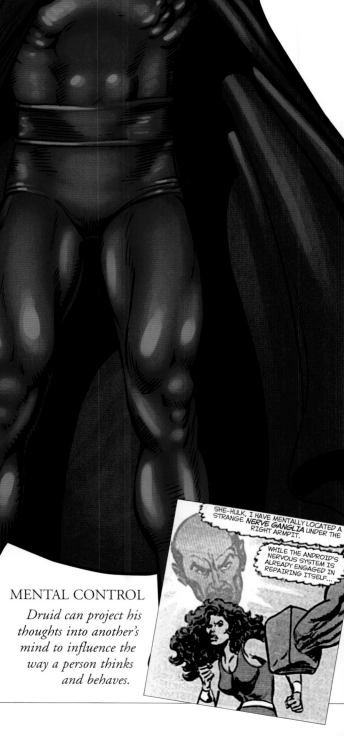

SHE-HULK, I HAVE MENTALLY LOCATED A STRANGE *NERVE GANGLIA* UNDER THE RIGHT ARMPIT.

WHILE THE ANDROID'S NERVOUS SYSTEM IS ALREADY ENGAGED IN REPAIRING ITSELF...

STARFOX

LOVE IS ALL YOU NEED according to Starfox. His real name is Eros and he grew up on Titan, one of the moons of Saturn. Eros spent most of his nearly immortal life as a fun-loving, partygoer, the exact opposite of his death-worshiping brother, Thanos. Eros began to rethink his life when his good friend Captain Mar-Vell died of cancer.

SOMETHING'S TROUBLING YOU, EROS! YOU'RE SO TENSE, SO RESTLESS!

CHANGED MAN
Shaken by Mar-Vell's death, Eros decided to use his superpowers for good.

HEAVEN-SENT HERO

After consulting ISAAC, Titan's master computer, Eros headed for Earth and joined the Avengers as Starfox. After the Vision was injured during a battle with the insectoid Annihilus, Starfox brought him back online by linking him with ISAAC. Starfox also helped the Avengers against Terminus, a gigantic alien trying conquer Earth.

The search for Nebula

...YES, THAT'S TRUE! I *MUST* FIND NEBULA...YOU SEE, SHE CLAIMS TO BE THE *GRAND-DAUGHTER* OF MY BROTHER THANOS!

GOOD LORD!

THERE MAY BE *NOTHING* TO HER CLAIM, BUT I MUST *KNOW* FOR CERTAIN!

On a mission to the Skrull Empire, Starfox learned that a vicious space pirate named Nebula was Thanos' granddaughter and his grandniece. Starfox carelessly let her escape the Avengers and resigned from the team to search the universe for her. He joined an army of heroes to confront Nebula, who possessed the Infinity Gauntlet, which held six "Infinity Gems" of vast power.

The Feel-Good Factor

Starfox possesses super-strength, the ability to levitate and telepathic powers. He can stimulate the pleasure centers in the minds of those near him, making an enemy feel so good that he stops fighting and surrenders!

Nebula

Like her grandfather Thanos, Nebula has always sought power. She attempted to seize control of the Skrull Empire and wiped out Skrull outposts and the planet Xander before the Avengers stopped her. She once gained superhuman powers through a brain implant that allowed her to channel all forms of energy, but Sersi managed to remove the device.

Nebula was caught by Starfox, but no prison could hold her long.

HIGHLY EVOLVED

The High Evolutionary's brain is so advanced that he has memorized all recorded human knowledge.

HERBERT WYNDHAM didn't think that evolution should be left to chance. He built a machine to accelerate evolution and experimented on animals, giving them humanlike intelligence. He also began to speed up his own evolution. Believing the people of Earth would never accept his "New Men," he built a space-ark to save them, like a latter-day Noah.

HEAR ME, MY FAITHFUL! FOR EVERY *KNIGHT* AMONG YOU, I HAVE PROVIDED YOU WITH A LADY TO TAKE AS YOUR *WIFE*.

GO FORTH INTO THE NEW CITY! BE FRUITFUL AND *MULTIPLY*. FROM HERE ON YOU SHALL BE RESPONSIBLE FOR REPLENISHING YOUR NUMBERS, FOR MY STORES OF YOUR *PROGENITORS* HAVE NOW BEEN *EXHAUSTED*!

GOD COMPLEX

Wyndham believed he was above nature itself, until he met Thor. While battling one of his own man-beasts alongside the Asgardian, the High Evolutionary realized that men might someday evolve into gods. He teamed up with the Hulk when his New Men tried to revolt against him and transformed himself into a godlike being.

The Evolutionary War

The High Evolutionary clashed with the Avengers when they learned he was plotting to set off a genetic bomb that would catapult the human race through a million years of evolution. They tracked him to a giant mobile base, where the Beast used a genetic accelerator on Hercules to make him powerful enough to defeat the Evolutionary.

Body armor contains all his genetic information and can restore him to life.

"IT WAS THEN THAT THE HIGH EVOLUTIONARY TOOK A MORE DIRECT HAND KNOWING OF A TRIBE OF GYPSIES CAMPED NEARBY HE ORDERED ME TO FETCH THE CHILDREN...

DIRECT ORDER
The Evolutionary ordered a gypsy shaman named Django Maximoff to raise the twins.

A Tale of Two Children

Years ago, a pregnant woman begged the Evolutionary for help. She said that her husband possessed great powers and planned a war against mankind. She had left him, fearing he would harm her unborn child. In time, she gave birth to twins, whom she left in the Evolutionary's care. The children grew up to be Quicksilver and the Scarlet Witch.

"...AND THEN, LIKE SOME MANIFESTING GOD, HE PLACED THEM IN THE CARE OF THE TRIBE'S SHAMAN, DJANGO MAXIMOFF AND HIS WIFE, WITH INSTRUCTIONS TO RAISE THE TWINS AS THEIR OWN.

"THE MAXIMOFFS WHO HAD RECENTLY LOST THEIR OWN CHILDREN --ANA AND MATEO-- COMPLIED.

GILGAMESH

HE IS THE LEGENDARY SLAYER of monsters. Like Sersi, Gilgamesh is an Eternal and has walked the Earth for centuries, doing battle with various threats to humanity. He toppled tyrants and slew the beasts men could not conquer. Many deeds attributed to the ancient heroes of myth were actually performed by Gilgamesh.

THE FORGOTTEN ONE

Zuras, leader of the Eternals, condemned Gilgamesh for the sin of pride and sent him into exile, casting a spell that erased him from everyone's memory. He journeyed into space and served the god-like Celestials. He eventually returned to Earth as their emissary and found himself in battle with the mighty Thor.

WIPED CLEAN

Like many of Gilgamesh's triumphs, his battle with Thor was wiped from the thunder god's memory.

The New Avenger

Gilgamesh heard that demons from another dimension had invaded New York City and Manhattan needed a monster-slayer. He joined an Avengers team comprising Thor, Mr. Fantastic, the Invisible Woman and Steve Rogers, then known as "The Captain."

Even Heroes Fall

After driving the demons away, Gilgamesh helped the Avengers in battles against Super-Nova, Puma and the U-Foes. He was also present when Avengers Island was propelled skyward by a column of molten rock. Surrounded by an army of Lava Men, Gilgamesh challenged a colossal lava-beast to single combat. A creation of magic, the creature disrupted Gilgamesh's virtually immortal body structure and almost beat him to death.

Without Equal
Gilgamesh is superhumanly strong and virtually immortal. His eyes or hands project cosmic energy and he has a vast knowledge of ancient combat techniques.

TRADITIONAL
COSTUME

Gilgamesh is so powerful he has no need of armor. He favors the humble attire of his namesake, an ancient Sumerian hero.

The FANTASTIC FOUR

REED RICHARDS and Susan Storm were engaged to be married when they embarked on a trip into space that changed their lives. Along with Ben Grimm and Sue's brother Johnny, they were exposed to cosmic radiation, which gave them amazing powers. Reed gained the ability to stretch his limbs to fantastic lengths. Sue could now turn invisible. Johnny could burst into flame like the Human Torch. Ben became the grotesque, super-strong Thing.

FOUR BECOMES THREE

Vowing to help mankind, the Fantastic Four was born. Three members of the FF, Reed and Sue Richards and the Thing, also served brief stints as Avengers.

The Avengers had disbanded after being betrayed by Doctor Druid so a new team was formed.

CHANGING TEAMS

After an argument with his teammates, the Thing joined the Unlimited Class Wrestling Federation and spent time in Los Angeles, where he occasionally aided the West Coast Avengers. After he returned to the FF, Reed and Sue took a leave of absence to raise their son. They joined a makeshift Avengers team to repel demons from another dimension, who were invading Manhattan.

Steve Rogers was simply known as "The Captain" at first.

The Flying Island
The new Avengers were Reed, Sue, Thor, Gilgamesh and Captain America. Reed and Sue saved Avengers Island (formerly known as Hydrobase) from total destruction when it was was suddenly propelled upward by a column of molten lava.

Forever Four
Like the Thing, Reed and Sue Richards did not remain with the Avengers for long. After leading the FF for so many years, Reed tended to disagree with Captain America over battle strategies. By mutual agreement, he and Sue returned to the Fantastic Four.

DEMOLITION MAN

DENNIS DUNPHY played football in high school and college, but wasn't good enough for a professional team. He heard about the Power Broker, who claimed to be able to give people superhuman strength. The process worked, but Dennis found that he was now far too strong to play football with normal humans!

GOOD BUDDIES

Having no other choice, Dennis joined the Unlimited Class Wrestling Federation where he became friends with Ben Grimm, alias the Thing.

The D-Man

After learning that some of the Power Broker's subjects became monsters, Dennis helped Captain America, one of his idols, end the experiments. Demolition Man, or "D-Man" as he was sometimes called, then became Cap's unofficial partner. Cap even invited Dennis to join the Avengers, but he never actually participated in any missions.

Dennis was a fan of Daredevil and based his costume on DD's first uniform.

AVENGERS CREW

EDWIN JARVIS, the Avengers' faithful butler, was severely injured when the new Baron Zemo and his Masters of Evil invaded the Avengers' Mansion. When he was released from the hospital, Jarvis realized that he could no longer perform all his regular duties. He needed help to maintain the mansion and keep all of the team's equipment in running order so he hired a support staff of interesting characters.

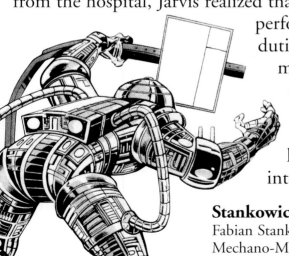

Stankowicz upgraded the Quinjets and the Mansion's defense systems.

Stankowicz & Carter

Fabian Stankowicz, formerly the Mechano-Marauder, became the team's staff inventor, technical advisor and repair specialist. Peggy Carter, who had dated Captain America during World War II, served as the communications officer.

O'Brien & Jameson

Former police detective Michael O'Brien was put in charge of security. Ex-astronaut John Jameson, became team pilot. He could transform into the super-powered Man-Wolf.

THE AVENGERS IN THE 1990s

THE NEW DECADE BEGAN with John Byrne still writing both Avengers titles. He was also drawing the West Coast book while penciler Paul Ryan and inker Tom Palmer handled the art for the East Coasters. Fabian Nicieza dropped in to write *The Crossing Line* in mid-1990, a thriller that involved a stolen nuclear submarine, Alpha Flight and a team of Russian super heroes. Larry Hama took over the scripting of the East Coast title and introduced new villains like Ngh the Unspeakable, and the Brethren and brought back old favorites like Doctor Doom and the Collector.

Roy Thomas returned to the Avengers in 1990 with a stint on the West Coast title that saw the team through *Operation: Galactic Storm* and clashes with Immortus, Ultron, and Goliath. Bob Harras and Steve Epting assumed creative control of the East Coast title in 1992 and brought back the Swordsman, made Hercules fall in love, forced the Black Knight to choose between Crystal and Sersi, and revealed the Gatherers' secret.

The title was discontinued in 1996 and Marvel hired Rob Liefeld and his studio to modernize the Avengers. It was later decided that Rob's stories occurred in a pocket universe and the Avengers were relaunched in 1998 under the creative guidance of Kurt Busiek, George Perez and Al Vey, who took a back-to-basics approach to the title.

The Avengers #350 (Aug. 1992) The X-Men and Starjammers help the Avengers celebrate their 350th issue. *(Cover by Steve Epting and Tom Palmer)*

The Avengers #360 (March 1993) The Avengers celebrate 30 years of continuous publication with a figure of the Vision embossed on a gold foil cover. *(Cover by Steve Epting and Tom Palmer)*

1990

The Avengers #314 (Feb. 1990) Spider-Man stops in for a visit as reality blinks out of existence. *(Cover by Paul Ryan)*

1992

The Avengers #348 (June 1992) The Vision and the Scarlet Witch say goodbye. *(Cover by Steve Epting and Tom Palmer)*

1993

Avengers: The Terminatrix Objective #1 (Sept. 1993) A four-issue series: Ravonna takes on Kang *(Cover by Mike Gustovich)*

1994

The Avengers #374 (May 1994) Proctor reveals his love and hatred for Sersi. *(Cover by Steve Epting and Tom Palmer)*

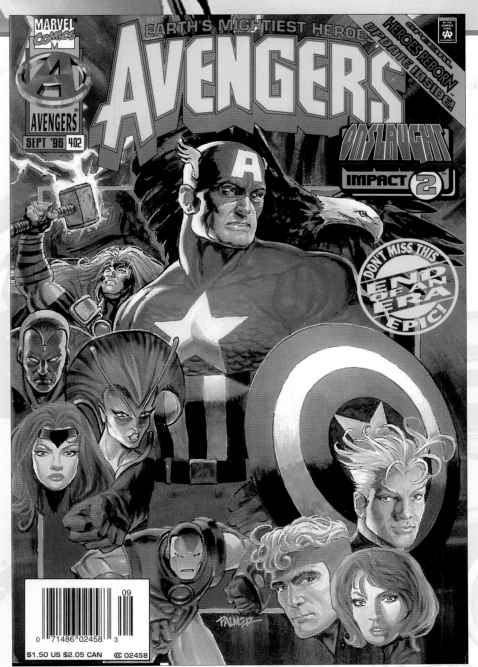

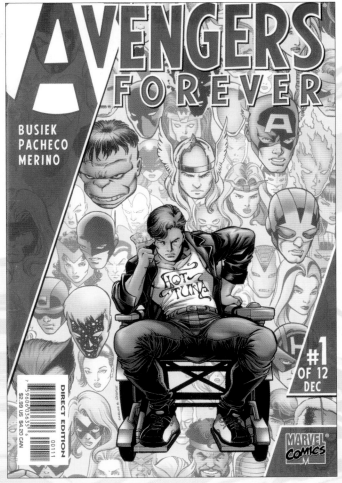

Avengers Forever #1 (Dec. 1998) Rick Jones is a major player in a twelve issue war between Kang and Immortus that revisits key moments in Avengers history. *(Cover by Carlos Pacheco and Jesus Merino)*

The Avengers #402 (Sept. 1996) The Avengers celebrate the end of an era as the first volume of the title draws to a close after 33 years. *(Cover by Tom Palmer)*

1995

The Avengers #387 (June 1995) The heroes team up with ghosts. *(Cover by Mike Deodato Jr.)*

1996

Avengers Vol. 2 #1 (Nov. 1996) The Avengers get a makeover. *(Cover by Rob Liefeld)*

1998

Avengers Vol. 3 #4 (May 1998) A new team is chosen. *(Cover by George Perez)*

1999

Avengers Vol. 3 #21 (Oct. 1999) The Avengers battle Ultron. *(Cover by George Perez)*

SO MANY OF THE CRASHERS WHO SHOW UP HERE TURN OUT TO BE CRASHING BORES, BUT I GET THE FEELING THAT YOU TWO ARE EXCEPTIONS AND *I LIKE EXCEPTIONS!*

I TAKE IT YOU KNOW THE GUILTY PARTIES, SHE-HULK ... WHY DON'T YOU INTRODUCE US?

SERSI

SERSI IS AN ETERNAL, a member of a race that is an evolutionary offshoot of humanity. All Eternals are virtually immortal and possess superhuman abilities. Sersi has always loved the pursuit of pleasure and has been throwing memorable parties since the beginning of recorded time. She was known as Circe in the days of ancient Greece.

REARRANGING REALITY

Sersi is able to mentally rearrange subatomic particles and transform any object into another. She can turn men into animals or boulders into boats. In ancient times, she met the Greek hero Odysseus and changed his sailors into pigs because they didn't behave at one of her parties.

IT'S TOO LATE TO RUN, YOU ARMOR-HEADED HALF-WITS! IT'S TIME YOU WERE *IMPROVED!*

Super Sorcery

Sersi also has considerable telepathic powers. She can scan the thoughts of anyone near her and project lifelike illusions into that person's mind. She also has the ability to teleport herself and others to any destination that she can visualize. Sersi's body is immune to disease and aging and she possesses superhuman strength and endurance.

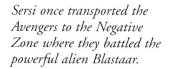

Sersi once transported the Avengers to the Negative Zone where they battled the powerful alien Blastaar.

Sersi can project cosmic energy from her eyes or hands

Sersi can levitate herself and others and can fly at nearly 800 mph (1,287 km/h).

Losing Her Mind

Sersi joined the Avengers to replace her fellow Eternal Gilgamesh, who had been seriously injured while battling the Lava Men. After linking her mind with the alien Brethren to stop them from devastating the Earth, Sersi began to experience temporary bouts of madness and had to be exiled from Earth.

Soulmates in Exile

Sersi flirted with Captain America, but she fell in love with the Black Knight. When Sersi learned that she was losing her mind and had to leave Earth, the Black Knight realized he loved her too much to let her go alone.

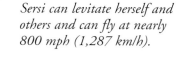

I AM TOO DANGEROUS TO LIVE.

THERE IS *NO* HOPE.

STINGRAY

DR. WALTER NEWELL was fascinated by the sea and its many secrets. An oceanographer employed by the U.S. government, he never intended to become a crime-fighting super hero. He built his Stingray suit simply to aid his studies, basing its design on the manta ray.

ISLAND REFUGE

Dr. Newell resides on Hydrobase, an artificial island in the Atlantic. When the authorities refused to allow the Avengers to land their Quinjets in New York City, Newell leased the team temporary aircraft storage space on his island.

Working Together
The Avengers and Stingray defended Hydrobase against the Super-Adaptoid, a synthetic creature able to mimic superhuman powers. Stingray also helped the Avengers defeat Russian terrorists, who had hijacked a nuclear submarine.

Stingray can fire an electric blast of 20,000 volts.

Undersea Power
Stingray wears an armored suit that enables underwater travel. He can dive to 1,200 ft (3,658 meters) and his oxygen-converting system provides an almost endless supply of air. The suit enables flight for short distances and gives Newell superhuman strength.

CRYSTAL

CRYSTALIA AMAQUELIN MAXIMOFF is an elemental, able to control fire, water, earth, and air. She is also a member of the Royal Family of the Inhumans, a genetically advanced race. She married Pietro "Quicksilver" Maximoff and they had a daughter named Luna.

Crystal was eager to prove herself.

Provisional Avenger
Crystal alerted the Avengers when an alien race called the Brethren materialized on Earth's moon. She joined the team in time to help them battle the Gatherers. Her relationship with hot-tempered Quicksilver began to fray, and Crystal became attracted to the Black Knight for a time, but she is still trying to make her marriage work.

The Nanny
Gruff, grumpy, and hugely strong, Marilla was chosen to become Luna's nanny by Black Bolt, monarch of the Inhumans.

WEB-BUSTING BATTLE
The Avengers involved Spidey in a clash with the super-powered space pirate Nebula.

SPIDER-MAN

PETER PARKER was an ordinary American teenager until a radioactive spider bit him and gave him the proportionate strength, speed, and agility of a spider. He also gained "spider-sense," which warned him of danger. At first he tried to cash in on his superpowers by becoming a television star. But when his uncle was murdered, he vowed to fight crime as Spider-Man.

One of Those Days
When Spider-Man offered to help Thor move some debris, the thunder god invited him to visit Avengers Mansion. Before long , the webhead was traveling across the galaxy, fighting space pirates and saving the universe!

FIRST FAILURE

Spider-Man was given the chance to join the Avengers—all he had to do was find the Hulk and bring him back to Avengers Mansion. After finding the Hulk, Spidey felt sorry for him when he learned he was really Bruce Banner, a tortured man unable to stop turning into the Hulk.

Second Failure
Learning that the Avengers each earned $1,000 a week, Spider-Man again asked for membership. When his request was denied, he crept aboard a Quinjet and was soon helping the team repel a Lava Men invasion. Spider-Man proved a useful ally, but the government wouldn't let him join the Avengers, viewing him as a security risk.

Fourth Time Lucky
Spider-Man later helped the Avengers track down Nebula, After she was defeated, he became a reserve member of the team. Spider-Man finally gained acceptance with the New Avengers, of which he is a valued member.

SANDMAN

IN A WAY, THE OTHER RESERVE SUBSTITUTE NEEDS NO REAL INTRODUCTION. YOU'VE KNOWN HIM FOR MANY YEARS AS THE *SANDMAN!*

WHILE ESCAPING PRISON, William Baker hid on a beach and was accidentally exposed to intense radiation. His body merged with the radioactive sand and he was transformed into a living Sandman. Baker was a criminal for many years, before her decided to reform. He was duly invited to become a reserve member of the Avengers.

HAVE TO DO A WHOLE LOT BETTER THAN THAT. SEE, I CAN MAKE MYSELF HARD AS ROCK --

SPEAKIN' OF *ROCKS,* LIKE THE ONE IN YOUR HEAD -- *LET US OUT!*

OUTTA AMMO -- DIDN'T PREPARE FOR *THINGS* LIKE HIM -- TIME TO SPLIT!

SAND TRAP

During his criminal days, the Sandman often fought Spider-Man. After going straight, he apologized to the webhead, and they became allies.

SEE WHY I'M CALLED THE *SANDMAN?!!*

Here's Sand in Your Eye!

The Sandman can convert all or part of his body into sand. He can also mold himself into any shape he can imagine. His fists can become huge rock-hard hammers or sharp weapons. He can slither beneath a door frame or slip through a foe's fingers. He can also fire his sand particles at high velocities.

MASQUE

COUNTESS GIULIETTA NEFARIA, daughter of Count Nefaria, took over his crime empire when he was jailed. Using the alias Whitney Frost, she tried to rob Stark Industries. The heist failed, however, and her face was scarred by chemicals during a plane crash.

The Midas Touch

Mordecai Midas, a power-hungry, ruthless criminal obsessed with gold, saved Giulietta's life and gave her a golden mask to hide her ruined face. An Olympic-level gymnast and athlete, martial artist and markswoman, she began working for Midas as Madame Masque.

WHICH IS EXACTLY WHAT *I* INTEND TO DO -- BUT AT *AVENGERS' MANSION,* WHERE THE REJUVENATION PROCESS CAN BE *MONITORED!*

NEFARIA MAY BE YOUR *FATHER,* WHITNEY --

BEHIND THE MASK

Because of her disfigured face, the loathsome Midas was the only man Masque felt comfortable with— until she met Tony Stark, alias Iron Man.

THEN BY ALL MEANS, LET US *DO SO ... TONIGHT!*

NATURALLY, MY DEAR, I TAKE *COMFORT* THAT YOU WILL BE ALONG IF ANYTHING SHOULD GO AMISS...

... TO *KILL* OUR FRIEND LEST HE MIGHT *TALK!*

DIVIDED LOVE

Iron Man's passion for Masque often led to him having to choose between her and his duty. Although Masque went on missions with the Avengers, she later rejoined her father.

LIVING LIGHTNING

SHOCK TACTICS
The Living Lightning can fly and discharge bolts of electrical power.

COSTUME SWITCH
Miguel's costume contains special devices that allow him to transform back to his human form with the speed of thought.

MIGUEL SANTOS was the son of a super-villain. His father belonged to a group of political extremists called the Legion of the Living Lightning that created a weapon that fired bolts of electricity. The Legion was destroyed and his father was killed in a battle with the Hulk. While searching the ruins of his father's headquarters, Miguel was exposed to his dad's lightning weapon and gained the ability to transform his body into electrical plasma.

PACIFIC MURDERERS

Intending to follow in his father's footsteps, Miguel joined Dr. Demonicus and his superhuman henchmen, the Pacific Overlords. Demonicus intended to raise an island from the depths of the Pacific Ocean to create his own nation. Miguel turned against the Overlords when he learned they were planning to murder a helpless hostage.

FIRST BATTLE
Shortly after he first gained his powers, Miguel attacked the original Human Torch, but was defeated by Dr. Hank Pym who rigged a device that drained his electrical power.

Reserve Status
Miguel joined the West Coast Avengers and encountered Arkon, a warlord from another dimension, and Titania, a warrior from a world ruled by women. He also aided the team against the giant demon named Satannish and a team of criminals with supernatural powers called the Night Shift. After fighting alongside the Avengers in the Kree-Shi'ar War, Miguel became a reserve member so that he could attend college.

MACHINE MAN

Any of Machine man's limbs can extend 100 ft (30.5 meters) in length.

X-51 WAS DESIGNED to be a killer. He was part of a government project to build robot soldiers that could make independent decisions. Believing that a robot could only act like a man if he was treated like one, Dr. Able Stack took one into his home and even designed a human face for him. The project was later terminated and only X-51 escaped destruction.

AGAINST ULTRON

Machine Man took on Ultron but failed to prevent the villain destroying his friend Jocasta.

Fighting For Love

X-51 agreed to battle the Avengers when the Super-Adaptoid, who could mimic anyone's superpowers, promised to rebuild Jocasta. To make amends, Machine Man later aided the West Coast Avengers.

DARKHAWK

WHILE EXPLORING an old amusement park, young Chris Powell found an amulet that gave him the ability to transform into Darkhawk, an android in a bio-mechanical suit with enhanced strength, speed, and agility. Chris fought with Spider-Man, Captain America and Daredevil and joined the teenage heroes the New Warriors.

WAY COOL!

Darkhawk could project blasts of dark energy, and his amulet could also generate defensive force-shields to protect him from harm.

Counterfeit Armor

Although based in New York City, Chris became a West Coast Avengers reserve when he helped them shut down Armor City, a place where fake Iron Man suits were being manufactured for criminals.

WINGS & CLAWS

Darkhawk possesses a pair of retractable glider wings that enable him to glide on wind currents for short distances. He also has a claw-cable on his right hand that can act as a grappling hook.

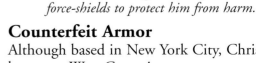

SPIDER-WOMAN 2

RACHEL, HONEY... YOU'RE REALLY OKAY, AREN'T YOU?

SURE. IT WAS SCARY-- BUT IT WAS FUN, TOO.

THAT'S GOOD. BUT NOW I--I'VE GOT SOMETHING TO TELL YOU-- ABOUT SPIDER-WOMAN.

SHE-- I MEAN-- I--

JULIA CARPENTER was desperate. She was a single mother and her ex-husband was a deadbeat. Bills were piling up, the rent was late, and her daughter Rachel had to be fed and clothed. Having no marketable skills, Julia volunteered to be a test subject for a government research project. One of the many injections she was given contained a serum created from spider venom. It somehow reacted with the other injections and Julia's own body chemistry to give her spider-like powers.

"THEN, ONE DAY, TWO INJECTIONS GOT MIXED UP SOMEHOW-- ON OF THEM HAD EXTRACTS FROM SPIDERS, THEY TOLD ME LATER--HEAVEN KNOWS WHY.

"WHEN THEY TOLD ME WHAT HAD HAP-PENED--

"WHEN THEY CAJOLED ME INTO LIFTING A SPORTS CAR OVER MY HEAD-- EVEN I BEGAN TO BE IMPRESSED.

"IT WAS A DAYTONA SPIDER, BY THE WAY.

"SOMEBODY'S IDEA OF A JOKE, I GUESS.

HAPPY ACCIDENT
Julia gained superhuman strength and agility. She could also leap 20 ft (6 meters) in one bound.

HONEST RELATIONSHIP
Julia revealed her secret identity to her daughter Rachel and even took her on some of her missions.

INTO ACTION

The first Spider-Woman had apparently retired, so Julia took the name. She met the Avengers when they were all transported to Battleworld, an artificial planet created for a series of secret wars by a being called the Beyonder. Returning to Earth, she joined Freedom Force, a government-sponsored team, and was told to arrest the Avengers.

UH-OH!

BUT SPIDER-WOMAN NONE-THELESS OBEYS. AGAIN AND AGAIN SHE LASHES OUT AT WONDER MAN'S HEAD UNTIL, FINALLY...

California Crime-fighter
Julia quit Freedom Force, moved to Los Angeles and took undercover solo work. Her investigations exposed the menace of the Pacific Overlords and she also helped the West Coast Avengers stop Dr. Demonicus. When Tigra left the team, Julia was nominated to replace her.

WE'VE BEEN WAITING FOR YOU, U.S. AGENT.

THAT'S TELLING HIM!

S-SPIT ON 'IM FOR ME, WILLYA, AGENT?

I'D DO IT MYSELF-- BUT MY THROAT'S STILL KINDA RAW.

THEN THAT MEANS... NOW YOU CAN ALL... TAKE A LONG WALK... OFF A SHORT PIER.

Julia joined the U.S. Agent and Hawkeye in a bid to capture the Hangman and his supernatural Night Shift gang.

Spider-Woman can project "psi-webs," and enough psionic energy through her hands and feet to crawl up walls.

RAGE

ELVIN DARYL HALIDAY was a short and skinny African-American child, who was often the butt of schoolyard bullies. He lived in Harlem and came from a poor, but honest family. While escaping some bigots who had accused him of stealing, he hid in a creek where a chemical company had illegally dumped radioactive material. The radiation triggered a genetic change in Elvin and he suddenly developed superhuman strength and a massive body.

RAGE-- DON'T!

I'VE HAD ENOUGH OF THIS CIRCUS-TRAINING!

SK RUMP

FIST OF VENGEANCE

Believing he had gained his powers to protect the helpless and punish the bullies of this world, Elvin became Rage. He demanded to join the Avengers because the team lacked an Afro-American member.

TEMPER TANTRUMS

The Avengers refused to let Rage join, but were impressed when he put a local drug dealer out of business. After aiding them against a gang of alien criminals, Rage was invited to become a reserve member. Captain America tried to teach him martial arts, but he kept losing his temper.

AND **ANOTHER** THING! HOW COME YOU'RE ALL DRESSED UP LIKE A **HOODLUM**? I CERTAINLY HOPE NONE OF THE **CHURCH LADIES** SAW YOU ALL DONE UP LIKE THAT.

THIS IS MY **COSTUME**, GRANNY! I'M A **SUPER HERO** NOW! UHH, CAN WE TALK ABOUT THIS SOME OTHER TIME, OR AT LEAST NOT AT THIS **VOLUME**?

GRANDMA STAPLES

Though Rage looked like an adult, his grandmother knew he was still a child and often scolded him—even in public. She disliked the fact that he wore a mask and was always so angry, but she still baked him cookies.

COSTUME? IT'S NOT **HALLOWEEN**! WHY ARE YOU WEARING A **MASK**? YOU GOT SOMETHING TO BE **ASHAMED** OF? I CERTAINLY HOPE NOT, YOU LIVING UNDER **MY** ROOF AND ALL! ONLY **HOODLUMS** WEAR MASKS, ELVIN--

SHHH! GRANNY, PLEASE--NOBODY'S SUPPOSED TO KNOW WHO I REALLY **AM**! AND CAN WE NOT BE DOING THIS IN FRONT OF THE **AVENGERS**--?

Hate Riots

The Hate Monger, a creature who fed off human hatred, allied with the Sons of the Serpent and ignited riots in New York City. Rage found himself paired with the teenage New Warriors, who helped him save Grandma Staples from the Serpents.

Rage is bulletproof and can stand up to the strongest blows.

Future Avenger

The Avengers were forced to expel Rage from their ranks when they discovered he was still a minor and so ineligible for membership. Undaunted, he switched to the New Warriors, which he preferred anyway. Though he is currently back in high school, Rage still plans to be an Avenger when he grows up

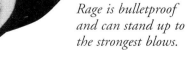

The GATHERERS

*T*HEY CAME FROM ravaged parallel Earths. Using a slash/way, a gateway into an alternate dimension, they journeyed across the multiverse, hunting the Avengers. Some they rescued; others, they simply murdered. It was their sacred responsibility to assemble all the Avengers worthy of life… for they were the Gatherers.

PROCTOR

The Gatherers' leader directed missions from a citadel hidden on the edge of reality. His team was unaware that Proctor had his own secret and very personal agenda.

ECHOES OF THE PAST

The Avengers became aware of the Gatherers when they were attacked by someone who appeared to be the long-deceased Swordsman. He was accompanied by a companion named Magdalene, a warrior armed with an energy lance that could open a slash/way.

The Gatherers were alternate world versions of the Avengers.

HANG BACK, HERKSTER -- -- I CAN HANDLE THIS OVERGROWN TEDDY BEAR!

More Monster Than Man

The Avengers later encountered Sloth, a giant, fur-covered creature with superhuman strength and razor-sharp claws, who may have been an alternate universe version of the Hulk or the Beast. Sloth was powerful enough to withstand a direct blow from Thor's enchanted hammer.

BY THE ALL-SEEING!

THEY HAVE *NEUTRALIZED* THE CLOAK! THEY CAN *SEE* US!

SLOTH, *DESTROY* THEM!

ALL-SEEING EYES

Cassandra was a blind and brilliant tactician who possessed the ability to foresee a number of possible futures and predict which one was the most likely to occur. She could also sense people and objects in her vicinity and instinctively knew how to move around or past them.

Proctor's Vengeance Quest

While the Watcher observed their final battle, the Avengers learned that Proctor had once loved the Sersi of his reality; however, she had driven him mad, leading him to kill every Avenger who had ever befriended her.

HEROES REBORN

IT BEGINS WITH ONSLAUGHT, a menace of pure psionic energy who wants to transform the entire human race into a single collective consciousness under his control. Banding with the Fantastic Four, the X-Men, and many other heroes, the Avengers have to sacrifice themselves to destroy Onslaught. But Earth's mightiest heroes are not really dead. They have simply been warped into a pocket universe where they have no memory of the past. They can thus become heroes reborn…

Ant-Man had a new armored look.

FAILED PROJECT

In this reality, Tony Stark designs the Iron Man armor as weapon he intends to sell to the military, but shelves the project when his best friend is killed during a test flight. Tony is later seriously injured in a helicopter crash and must don the armor to save himself and prevent the Hulk destroying the man who created him: Dr. Bruce Banner, his own alter ego.

Fresh Challenges, Familiar Foes
In this reality, the Avengers are funded by the government and report directly to Nick Fury, the commander-in-chief of S.H.I.E.L.D. Peter Gyrich is their official liaison officer and the team's base of operations is an entire island in Manhattan Bay. The New Avengers team face a couple of old foes: Kang the Conqueror comes from the future, filled with desire to win the heart of Mantis; and Asgardian mischief-maker Loki suspects that something is wrong with this universe and realizes that the Avengers are the key to the mystery.

AVENGERS ASSEMBLE
Led by Captain America, the new team consists of Hellcat, Hawkeye, Scarlet Witch (who is secretly the daughter of the Enchantress), Swordsman, and Vision. The team free Thor, who has been frozen in ice for centuries.

A NEW LETHAL LEGION
Seeking to reshape the new universe in his own image, Loki convinces the Enchantress to form a new Lethal Legion, with Wonder Man, Executioner, and Ultron V.

MORGAN LE FEY

SHE SUFFERED FROM a bad case of sibling rivalry. Morgan Le Fey's half-brother was King Arthur of Camelot and she was only half human. Though she and Arthur shared the same mother, her father was believed to have been a member of an ancient magical race that once inhabited Britain. After learning the arts of sorcery, Morgan plotted against King Arthur until Merlin the Magician cast a spell that imprisoned her within the walls of Castle Le Fey.

HEADING FOR A FALL
After luring Spider-Woman into the past for a showdown, Morgan fell out one of the castle windows and her body was obliterated by Merlin's magic spell.

ASTRAL PROJECTION

However Morgan, one of the most powerful sorceresses in history, was not to be so easily confined. Although her body couldn't leave the castle, her astral form was free to travel to various time periods as she searched for a way to free herself. Morgan fastened upon Jessica Drew, the first Spider-Woman, believing that she could use her to break Merlin's spell. When Spider-Woman refused to aid her, Morgan tried to destroy her.

EXCALIBUR
Sending her spirit into the present, Morgan used her dark sorcery to transform a simple thief into a sword-swinging superhuman who called himself Excalibur.

MONUMENTAL MAGIC
Morgan's spirit journeyed to the present and tried to possess Spider-Woman's body. When the Avengers entered the astral plane to stop her, Morgan created a gigantic stone-like body for herself. The team smashed this, with help from Doctor Strange, but Morgan's spirit continued searching for a new home.

The Morgana Quest
Having stolen the Twilight sword, a weapon of monumental power, Morgan kidnapped the Scarlet Witch. The sorceress used Wanda's incredible reality-altering powers to recreate a distorted version of Camelot, in which the Avengers served as her knights. Captain America managed to break free from the spell and led a revolt the soon freed other Avengers and restored reality.

JUSTICE & FIRESTAR

VANCE ASTROVIK dreamed of being an astronaut; but when he dicovered he was a mutant with telekinetic powers, he resolved to become an Avenger. Vance can levitate himself, move objects with his mind and project psionic blasts. Angelica Jones was also a mutant. Recruited by the Massachusetts Academy, a school for young mutants, she received the code name Firestar and learned to control her ability to project heat and manipulate microwaves.

SECURITY ALERT
Vance ran into problems when he arrived at Avengers Mansion without an appointment.

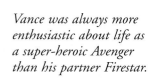

Vance was always more enthusiastic about life as a super-heroic Avenger than his partner Firestar.

WARRIORS TOGETHER

Calling himself Marvel Boy, Vance applied for membership with the Avengers, but was turned down because of his age. He later joined a team of teenage heroes called the New Warriors that consisted of Night Thrasher, Speedball, Namorita, Nova, and Firestar. Vance and Angela fell in love, and he changed his name to Justice.

Reluctant Avenger
The New Warriors helped the Avengers fend off an attack by the Sons of the Serpent. Justice later persuaded Firestar to try out for the Avengers, but she was none too keen.

Love is Enough
After a vicious battle with Whirlwind, Justice and Firestar were offered status as reserve members. They aided the team against the Squadron Supreme, the Kree and the Legion of the Unliving before returning to college and focusing on their relationship.

SILVERCLAW

MARIA DE GUADALUPE SANTIAGO was a mutant who could transform into a strange beast. Raised in the tiny country of Costa Verde, her father claimed that her mother was the legendary volcano goddess Peliali, protector of the people. He took Maria to the caves beneath the sleeping volcano, but they never found Peliali.

I AM NO MERE *WERECAT*, CAPTAIN! I AM *LA GARRA ARGENTADO* -- AND *ALL* THE JUNGLE'S ASPECTS LIVE IN *ME!*

IF THE STEALTH OF THE *JAGUAR* WAS NOT SUFFICIENT TO BEAT YOU, THEN THE WINGS OF THE *COCKATOO* WILL CARRY ME ABOVE YOUR LUNGE --

-- AND THE STRENGTH OF THE *ANACONDA* --

-- WILL CRUSH THE *BREATH* FROM YOU!

HOKK!

JUNGLE QUEEN
Shape-shifting Silverclaw can call upon the powers of any jungle beast. She can also employ multiple animal powers at the same time.

A LONELY ORPHAN

After her father grew sick and died, Maria was taken in by a church orphanage. The priests were nervous about her powers and kept her away from the other children. She had no friends until a letter arrived from America. Edwin Jarvis had responded to an ad and became Maria's sponsor. He eventually arranged for her to come to New York to attend school and that is when he discovered she was secretly Silverclaw.

EDWIN JARVIS, I'D LIKE YOU TO MEET *MARIA DE GUADALUPE SANTIAGO* -- A.K.A. *SILVERCLAW.*

I -- SHE -- YOU --

HOLA, *TIO* EDWIN. ARE YOU -- ARE YOU *MAD* AT ME--?

When Maria becomes Silverclaw, she gains the speed and agility of a jungle cat.

Silverclaw combined the speed and agility of a monkey with the power of Jaguar to overcome the wizard Gath Toth.

Hijack
A team of heavily armed terrorists attempted to hijack the plane that carried Maria to America, forcing her to transform herself into the ferocious Silverclaw. During the confusion of battle, she attacked Captain America and later had to apologize to him and the Avengers.

MAD AT YOU? WHY, CHILD, I COULDN'T *POSSIBLY* BE--

-- OH!

NOW, NOW, CHILD -- THERE'S NO NEED TO *CRY*--!

ALL FORGIVEN
Maria was fearful that Jarvis would now reject her for being a freak, but he quickly put her mind at ease.

GHUHH!

TRIATHLON

DELROY GARRETT, JR. grew up in the suburbs of Philadelphia. A natural athlete, he ran track in high school and broke every record. He began training for the Olympics, but then started to doubt his talent. The pressure to win overcame his better judgment and he began taking steroids to improve his performance. He won three gold medals and was offered a fortune in endorsement contracts—until he was caught out by a routine drugs test.

Delroy was everyone's hero until he was caught cheating in the Olympic Games.

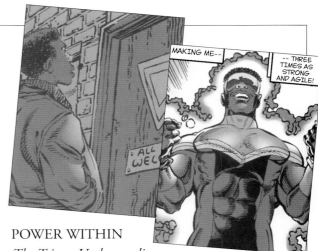

POWER WITHIN
The Triune Understanding showed Delroy how to unlock the latent power within himself, enhancing his strength, speed and agility to almost superhuman levels.

A NEW PATH

Stripped of all his medals, banned from all competition, Delroy fell into a deep depression. Then he discovered the Triune Understanding, a cult that claimed to have a new holistic approach. The Triune Understanding showed Delroy how to banish his shame and self-hatred and unlock his full physical potential.

POWER PUNCH
Triathlon was strong enough to help Captain America and the Avengers subdue Silverclaw.

Triathlon could run fast enough to dodge bullets.

Making the Team
Triathlon learned that Moses Magnum intended to steal a seismic cannon and led the Avengers to Magnum's base. Triathlon also joined the Avengers in battle against the Grim Reaper, Kang, and the Presence, a former Soviet scientist who could generate nuclear energy within his own body.

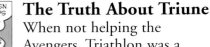

The Truth About Triune
When not helping the Avengers, Triathlon was a spokesman for the Triune Understanding until he discovered it was a front for Lord Templar, a terrorist posing as a champion of peace.

A-NEXT

*I*N A POSSIBLE FUTURE that may never occur, the Avengers learn of a major threat to Earth. Many Avengers die or are seriously injured in the battle that follows. The Earth is saved but the team is left in ruins and eventually disbands. Years pass and Avengers Compound becomes a tourist attraction, but Edwin Jarvis believes that the Avengers will return someday…

A new team of Avengers rises from the ashes of the old. Speedball doesn't join the team, but the former New Warrior helps them on their first case.

STINGER

J2

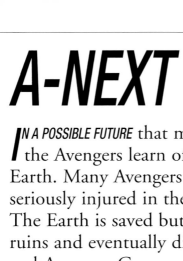

MY DAD'S ENCHANTED MACE-- *THUNDERSTRIKE!*

BUT I THOUGHT IT WAS DESTROYED YEARS AGO!

OBVIOUSLY NOT.

WHAT'S THE DEAL? AM I SUPPOSED TO PICK UP WHERE DAD LEFT OFF?

THERE WAS A TIME I DREAMED OF BEING A *SUPER HERO* -- EVEN DESIGNED A *COSTUME* FOR MYSELF!

THUNDERSTRIKE

Kevin Masterson, son of the deceased Eric, returns to New York City and learns that Jarvis has been holding his father's enchanted mace for him. When Loki tries to steal the mace, Kevin is magically merged with it and becomes Thunderstrike, able to fire bolts of energy from his hands.

SPEEDBALL

SLIPPING INTO A SECLUDED SPOT ZANE BEGINS A TO *CONCENTRATE!* CONCENTRATE! CONCENTRATE!

THROUGH A SHEER ACT OF WILL HE SOON AFFECTS A TRANSFORMATION OF HIS OWN, BECOMING THE ALMIGHTY *J2!*

FOR DETAILS ON HIS ORIGIN, CHECK OUT *J2#1!* ON SALE IN ONLY THE FINEST COMIC SHOPS!

MAINFRAME

J2

Zane Yama is the son of Cain Marko, the original Juggernaut, and his wife Sachi Yama, an Assistant District Attorney. His parents met after Marko was pardoned for his past crimes and joined the X-Men. Long after Marko disappears while on a mission, Zane learns that he can mentally transform himself into an almost unstoppable Juggernaut.

MAINFRAME

Mainframe is not a real person: he is a sophisticated computer program based on the encephalograms of Tony Stark. Built so that there would always be an Avenger to protect the Earth, he can download his consciousness into a new body whenever necessary.

THE NAME IS *MAINFRAME!*

I HAVE LITTLE REGARD FOR *BULLIES,* AND EVEN LESS FOR *THREATS!*

Jubilee is now the leader of the X-People, but she often aides the new Avengers team.

JUBILEE

THUNDERSTRIKE

Stinger

Adventurous Cassandra Lang is the daughter of Scott Lang, formerly Ant-Man. She helps her dad run Langlabs, a full-service think tank. Using principles developed by Hank Pym, they develop an armored suit that allows her to fly, to shrink to insect size, fire bio-blasts and communicate with insects. Stinger becomes the leader of the new Avengers.

MISSION COMMANDER! YOU SURVIVED THE CRASH!

Uhhhh... SURE! LET'S GO WITH THAT FOR NOW!

SENTRY 666, YOU ARE HEREBY ORDERED TO CEASE ALL CONFLICT! OUR MISSION IS TERMINATED!

Earth Sentry

John Foster is the son of Bill Foster, who often assisted Hank Pym and eventually became the new Goliath. When a Kree Sentry arrives on Earth, John accidentally triggers a device that transforms his genetic structure, making him part Kree. He gains superhuman strength, the ability to fly and project blasts of cosmic energy.

IT LOOKS LIKE WE'VE BEEN REPLACED BY A WHOLE NEW TEAM!

RIVAL HEROES

Trained by Hawkeye, the Dream Team—American Dream, Freebooter, Bluestreak, and Crimson Curse—eventually becomes part of the new Avengers team.

Deathcry

After learning that their age-old enemies the Kree had sent a team of assassins to Earth, the alien race known as the Shi'ar sent one of their top warriors to apprehend them: Deathcry. Her wrist-bands fired 8-in (20-cm) quills that telescoped into a variety of javelins, releasing electrical charges or sleep-inducing fumes on impact. An arrogant military strategist who hated all things Kree, Deathcry alerted the Avengers, helped them round up the Kree warriors and stayed with the team until the Shi'ar recalled her.

ALL TOO MUCH

With her bulging biceps and wild hair, Deathcry was an awe-inspiring sight. She was keen to strike up a close relationship with the Vision, but the sensitive android soon had second thoughts.

THE AVENGERS IN THE 2000s

HAVING RESTORED Earth's Mightiest Heroes to fan-favorite status, Kurt Busiek and George Perez explored the Triune Understanding, included Triathlon in the lineup, explored Silverclaw's origin, and revived Madame Masque and Count Nefaria. The Avengers also participated in a major crossover in late 2000 called *Maximum Security*, drawn by John Romita, Jr., in which alien empires tried to transform Earth into a prison planet.

In 2001, Kurt Busiek finished his run with a 16-issue epic in which Kang established his dynasty. Mark Millar and Bryan Hitch took a new approach with the launch of the acclaimed Ultimates in 2002, and in the regular Avengers title, Geoff Johns and Kieron Dwyer produced a story in which the Avengers were asked to rule the world. Johns later wrote *The Search for She-Hulk*, in which Jennifer Walters runs amok. Chuck Austin brought back Morgan Le Fey and the Wrecking Crew. He also introduced a new Captain Britain and Invaders. The Avengers disassembled at the end of 2004.

During 2005, the Great Lakes Avengers received a four-issue series, courtesy of Dan Slott and Paul Pelletier; Allan Heinberg and Jim Cheung introduced the world to the Young Avengers; and Brian Michael Bendis and David Finch reassembled a team of New Avengers that included Spider-Man and Wolverine.

Avengers #503 (Dec. 2004) After seismic upheavals, the Avengers finally call it quits. *(Cover by David Finch)*

Avengers Vol. 3 #25 (Feb. 2000) A number of old friends and older enemies drop in to celebrate the Avengers return to greatness at the hands of Kurt Busiek and George Perez. *(Cover by George Perez)*

2000

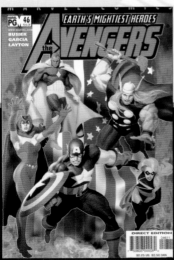

Avengers Vol. 3 #31 (August 2000) The Vision returns with the Grim Reaper and Madame Masque. *(Cover by George Perez)*

2001

Avengers Vol. 3 #46/ Vol. 1 #463 (Nov. 2001): Kang conquers the whole Earth. *(Cover by Kieron Dwyer)*

2002

Avengers Vol. 3 #50/ Vol. 1 #465 (March 2002) Kang enslaves the Avengers. *(Cover by Kieron Dwyer)*

2003

Avengers Vol. 3 #69/ Vol. 1 #484 (Sept. 2003) A toxic chemical is released over Mount Rushmore.

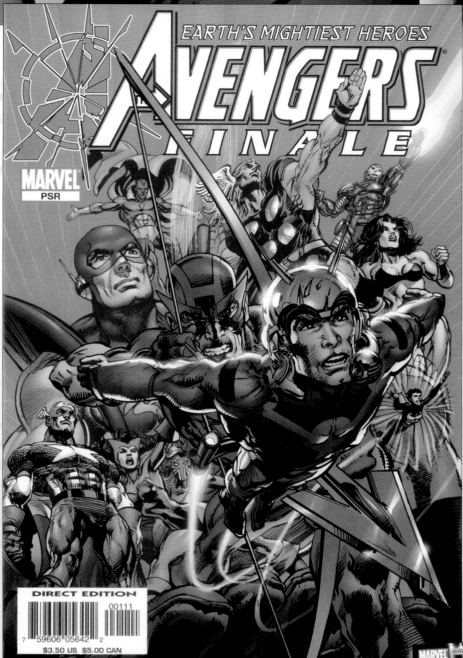

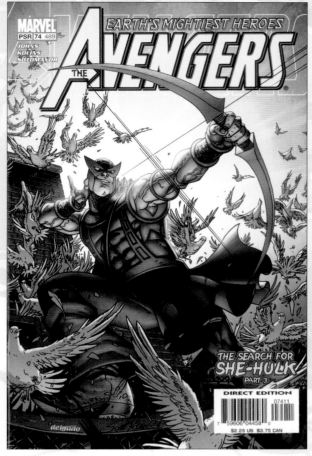

Avengers Vol. 3 #74/ Vol. 1 #489 (Jan. 2004)
Hawkeye joins the search for the missing She-Hulk.
(Cover by Mike Delgado)

Avengers Finale (Jan. 2005) The surviving
Avengers gather together to reminisce and bid
goodbye to each other. *(Cover by Neal Adams
and Laura Martin)*

2004   **2005**

*Avengers Vol. 3 #80/ Vol. 1 #495
(May 2004)* A new Captain
Britain is born. *(Cover by David
Finch and Art Teibert)*

*Earth's Mightiest Heroes #1 (Jan.
2005)* An eight-issue celebration
of all things Avengers. *(Cover by
Scott Kolins)*

New Avengers #1 (Jan. 2005) & #4 (April 2005)
A new tradition begins with a new team and name, and
the New Avengers travel to the Savage Land and meet
Wolverine.*(Covers by David Finch and Danny Miki)*

--BUT THE REASON I ORIGINALLY TOOK YOUR OFFER TO BE ANT-MAN WAS BECAUSE I CRAVED EXCITEMENT AND ADVENTURE, AND IF THAT MEANS BEING DOCKED AN HOURS PAY, PAL, THEN THEMS THE BREAKS!

ANT-MAN 2

SCOTT LANG WANTED to be a good father. An electronics expert, he turned to crime to help pay the bills and support his family. He was eventually arrested and sent to prison. Paroled for good behavior, he got a job at Stark Industries, but his wife divorced him, giving him custody of their daughter Cassie. Scott then learned that Cassie needed an expensive heart operation and that her surgeon had been kidnapped!

Ant-Man's helmet has its own air supply. It gives him all-round vision and the ability to communicate with ants.

TO SAVE HIS DAUGHTER

Desperate to rescue the surgeon and save Cassie's life, Scott broke into the home of Dr. Hank Pym and stole his old Ant-Man costume and shrinking formula. Scott became a new Ant-Man and freed the surgeon, who then operated on Cassie.

WOK

YEAH. JUST LIKE BURT REYNOLDS BOPPING ROBERT KLEIN IN "HOOPER"!

The Ant Avenger

Willing to go to jail for his crime, Scott returned the Ant-Man outfit to Pym. Pym revealed that he had been following Scott as Yellowjacket and offered to allow him to continue as Ant-Man.

Scott accepted and helped the Avengers battle the Absorbing Man (*above*) and his girlfriend Titania.

Let's take a peek --

--inside.

Shrink to Fit

Ant-Man usually stands one-half-inch tall, but he can make himself small enough to enter a sub-atomic microverse. He can also shrink other people and objects.

Ant Muscle

Scott helped to rescue Yellowjacket and the Wasp from the Taskmaster, a criminal with the ability to mimic anyone's physical abilities. After a brief consulting stint with the Fantastic Four, Scott joined the Avengers and was pivotal in apprehending Scorpio (*right*), a member of the Zodiac crime cartel.

Harsh Verdict

Scott paid a high price for Avengers membership. His ex-wife learned that he was the new Ant-Man and had moved Cassie into the Avengers Mansion. Fearing for her safety, she took Scott to court and he lost custody of his daughter.

Don't make this harder than it has to be Mr Lang.

Daddy!

JACK OF HEARTS

JACK HART WAS THE SON of a brilliant scientist who invented an incredibly efficient, inexpensive liquid fuel called Zero Fluid. Jack's father intended to make it available to all the free countries in the world. Criminals tried to steal the formula, killing Jack's father and dousing Jack with the only existing sample.

Zero Fluid
Blaming himself for failing to save his father, Jack was determined to hunt down anyone connected to the gang—leading to clashes with the authorities, and with super heroes.

An explosive personality
The highly corrosive fuel permanently scarred Jack's body and caused mutagenic changes. He began to generate incredible bursts of "zero energy," which he could expel in the form of blasts of intense heat. He could also use it to fly. His energy increased and he designed a protective armored suit to contain it. When even this began to fail, he exiled himself to space. He recently returned and asked the Avengers for help.

THE ZERO ROOM
To prevent himself from exploding like an atomic bomb, Jack must spend 14 hours a day in the Mansion's "Zero Room", which siphons off his excess energy.

CAPTAIN BRITAIN

BORN AND RAISED in London, Kelsey Leigh was an English teacher and mother of two. She was attacked one night while with her husband. He did nothing, but she fought back and received a cruel facial scar. Their marriage ended soon after.

The Wrecking Crew
Morgan le Fey learned the Avengers were visiting England. She placed a spell on the costumed criminals known as the Wrecking Crew and sent them to attack the heroes. Kelsey and her children were caught in the fight. Captain America was seriously injured trying to protect them and Kelsey sacrificed her life to save his.

The legendary hero Captain Britain and his wife appeared to Kelsey, offering her the chance to defend England against evil.

SWORD OF VENGEANCE
Kelsey seized the chance to become a modern-day Captain Britain. She now possessed super-strength and was armed with an magic sword that could transform into a battle-staff and discharge blasts of psionic energy. She had soon taken revenge on her killer.

AVENGERS DISASSEMBLED

IT SEEMED LIKE ANY OTHER DAY at Avengers Mansion. Jarvis was serving breakfast as Hawkeye and Scott Lang discussed women foes they found attractive. Suddenly a perimeter alarm sounded, indicating a security breach. Jack of Hearts was standing in the gardens. Scott went to greet him and Jack apologized—before suddenly releasing his Zero Energy in an explosion that incinerated Scott and wrecked the Mansion!

HUMILIATED

At that very moment, Iron Man Tony Stark was addressing the United Nations. He suddenly started acting as if he were drunk and threatened to murder the Latverian delegate. Tony's mortification following his outrageous rant is mixed with bewilderment, for he is certain that he hasn't had anything to drink!

Fatal Vision

Moments later, a Quinjet crashed into the Mansion. Stepping from the wreckage, the Vision announced that he could no longer control the organisms that made up his and he begins to self-destruct.

ULTRON ARMY

As the Vision's body dissolved, he ejected five metal capsules. As soon as they hit the ground, they became five Ultron robots, which immediately attacked the remaining Avengers.

Wild and Crazy

During the battle that follows, the She-Hulk turned savage and lost her sanity. She battled friend and foe alike, severely injuring both the Wasp and Captain America before Iron Man brought her down. While the team tried to regroup, every costumed crime-fighter who was ever a member showed up to support them.

The heroes were soon attacked by a Kree strikeforce....

...and Hawkeye laid down his life for the team.

> BUT I THOUGHT BY NOW YOU WOULD UNDERSTAND THE TRUE NATURE OF THESE ATTACKS.

> THE MAGICS ARE BEING ABUSED.

BY OUR OWN BETRAYED

Doctor Strange, sorcerer supreme, suddenly arrived on the scene. Having sensed that an abuse of great magics was taking place, he knew there was only one person who could have orchestrated such incredible chaos—Wanda Maximoff, the Scarlet Witch! Strange believed that Wanda had fallen victim to her own power, a power that she had never fully comprehended

> MOMMY, DON'T LET THEM TAKE US AWAY.

> NO. IT WON'T HAPPEN AGAIN.

> MOMMY, I DON'T WANT TO GO AWAY AGAIN!

> NO ONE WILL TAKE YOU AWAY FROM ME AGAIN.

A Deadly Dream

Captain America entered Wanda's fantasy world, where she was still married to the Vision and living happily with their two children. She conjured up super-menaces to protect her dream, prepared to kill anyone who opposed her.

> YOU WILL STOP THIS MADNESS NOW.

> YOU ARE HURTING YOUR FRIENDS AND HURTING YOURSELF!

> THIS STOPS *NOW!*

The Curtain Falls

The battle ended when Doctor Strange (above) employed the mystical Eye of Agamotto to shock Wanda back to reality. As she sank into a coma, Magneto arrived to fetch her. Having lost so much, the team decided the time had come to disband. They bade farewell to the city they had protected for so many years. The saga of the Avengers was finally over... or was it?

SENTRY

Sentry could generate psionic blasts or protective force-fields.

HE WAS HUMANITY'S shining guardian in the face of an impossible storm, an untouchable hero-god who radiated confidence and courage. Bob Reynolds believed that he was one of the first costumed superhumans of the modern age, predating even the Fantastic Four. He possessed the psionic power of a million suns. He was super-strong, super-fast, able to fly and practically invulnerable. But no one remembers him. It's as if he never existed. Maybe he didn't.

> WHY ARE YOU HOLDING BACK, SENTRY? AM I NOT EVERYTHING YOU FEARED AND MORE?
>
> ARE YOU NOT AFRAID?

'I REMEMBER THE SENTRY STOOD BEFORE US... NOT DEFIANT, BUT *PROUD*. EVERYONE NOW KNEW THAT HE AND THE VOID WERE ONE AND THE SAME PERSON.

' BUT THERE HE WAS -- THIS MAN WHO'D SUBCONSCIOUSLY KILLED A MILLION PEOPLE, DESTROYED HALF A CITY... HE WAS THE SAME MAN WHO'D SAVED A HUNDRED MILLION MORE.

THE VOID

Sentry's archenemy was the Void, a superhuman menace who was always trying to destroy the Earth. Sentry eventually realized that the Void was a dark manifestation of his own subconscious. In order to eliminate the Void, Sentry psionically erased his existence from everyone's mind… including his own.

Carnage

Sentry was wrongly jailed for killing his wife. He escaped but was attacked by Carnage, a serial killer. Sentry dispersed the creature in space, unwittingly freeing the Void by using his powers again.

Convinced that he had murdered his wife, Sentry rotted away his life in prison.

Telepathic Remedy

Captain America was convinced the world could do with a hero like Sentry. He hunted him down and introduced him to Emma Frost, a powerful mutant telepath. She peered into Sentry's mind and learned that many of his beliefs were false: he had been the victim of some kind of psychic brainwashing.

COMEBACK

After learning that his wife still lived and that he could always keep the Void in check, Sentry joined the new Avengers and renewed old acquaintances.

SPIDER-WOMAN

JESSICA DREW was born to an American anthropologist and his British wife. Her father worked closely with Herbert Wyndham, the High Evolutionary. As a child, Jessica was exposed to radioactive uranium, and her father injected her with a serum composed of irradiated spider's blood, hoping to save her life. When she still failed to recover, the High Evolutionary used his genetic accelerator on her.

SIDE-EFFECTS
Jessica's mother died suddenly and her father fell into a deep depression, so the High Evolutionary supervised her treatment. He was surprised to find that his accelerator had caused the spider serum to mutate within her body.

INCREDIBLE! THE ACCELERATOR'S BUILDING ON JOHN'S SERUM -- IN WAYS I NEVER *EXPECTED*.

LAD, THE *LASER'S* NOT STOPPING HER. IT'S NOT *STRONG* ENOUGH!

ZDAK!

MY *VENOM BLAST* SHOULD PUT THAT ONE AWAY FOR A WHILE...

FREELANCE AGENT
Jessica began to date a young man and accidentally discharged a bioelectric blast that almost killed him. Jessica fled the scene and became a fugitive from justice. The terrorist group H.Y.D.R.A. learned of her powers and sent her to kill Nick Fury. He persuaded her to switch sides and join S.H.I.E.L.D. When not working for Fury, Jessica worked as a bounty hunter and, later, as a private detective.

VENOM BLASTS
Not only is Spider-Woman immune to radiation and poison, she can also generate concussive blasts of bioelectric energy.

UH-HUH, LADY--

ZADT!

Spider Power
Spider-Woman has superhuman strength and agility. She can stick to walls by excreting an adhesive substance from her hands and feet and can fly. She is also a skilled martial artist and trained in espionage techniques.

Double Trouble
When H.Y.D.R.A. tried to blackmail her into becoming a double agent, Jessica immediately told Nick Fury, who insisted she take the deal and turn the tables on them. Jessica was working for S.H.I.E.L.D. when Captain America invited her to join the new Avengers.

Spider-Woman radiates pheromones that attract men and repel women.

NEW AVENGERS

AGENT JESSICA DREW of S.H.I.E.L.D. was assigned to escort blind lawyer Matt Murdoch and his bodyguard Cage to a maximum security prison to question Sentry, a super hero who believed he had murdered his wife. No sooner did they enter the prison, than a jailbreak occurred, freeing 87 of the world's most dangerous criminals. Captain America, Iron Man, and Spider-Man soon arrived to quell the riot, and a new team of Avengers was born—with new members.

WHEN WE CLOSED THE MANSION...

LISTEN--THERE'S THIS-- A *BALANCE* TO THE CITY, TO THE COUNTRY, THAT WE INADVERTENTLY, BY ENDING THE AVENGERS...

...*WE* THREW THE BALANCE OUT OF WHACK.

A TEAM *NEEDS* TO BE IN A PLACE.

THINGS LIKE THIS-- WHAT HAPPENED LAST NIGHT--

THIS IS *EXACTLY* WHY THERE NEEDS TO BE AN AVENGERS.

IT THE OLD AVENGERS DON'T WANT TO, IF THEY CAN'T, THEN LET'S TRY THESE NEW ONES.

CAGE UNCAGED

Hero for hire Luke Cage was once framed and sent to prison. In order to obtain early parole, he volunteered to be a test subject for an experimental chemical. An angry guard tried to kill Cage by giving him an overdose. Instead of killing him, the drug reacted with Cage's unique body chemistry and gave him superhuman strength.

Ronin

Once called Echo because of her ability to copy any physical move she saw, Maya Lopez, alias Ronin, is a skilled martial artist and weapons expert. She is also deaf and Daredevil's girlfriend. He recommended her to Captain America.

AVENGERS TOWER

Located ten blocks from the Fantastic Four's Baxter Building, the Avengers' new headquarters is an office tower owned by Tony Stark.

Saga of Sauron

The jailbreak was arranged by a mutant group called the Savage Land Mutates. Their goal was to free Karl Lykos, who drained energy from his victims to transform into Sauron, a winged reptile with hypnotic powers. The Avengers tracked Lykos to the Savage Land, a jungle inhabited by dinosaurs. There they encountered the X-Man Wolverine, who helped the team defeat the mutates and capture Lykos. The Avengers also uncovered an illegal S.H.I.E.L.D. operation to mine weapons-grade vibranium using slave labor.

PULLING TOGETHER

Membership of the new team is fluid. Any hero who has ever been an Avenger may be present at meetings, as may luminaries such as Dr. Strange, Reed Richards, Professor Xavier, Black Bolt and Namor.

Wolverine

Wolverine was invited to join the new team with the understanding that he could continue his membership in the X-Men. Logan is a mutant who possesses a healing factor which enables him to recover from almost any injury. It also retards aging. He has superhumanly acute senses and his skeleton has been artificially reinforced with adamantium. His help was crucial when the Avengers were beset by dinosaurs in the Savage Land *(below)*.

Wolverine has three natural claws on each hand which have also been sheathed in adamantium. They can cut through almost anything and be triggered or withdrawn in an instant.

RRAAAGGHHRRR

Man, heading S.H.I.E.L.D. is like being the Pope, the Queen and the President of the United States all rolled into one, Doctor Banner.

The ULTIMATES

conventional numbers and reinvesting in a small, *Superhuman Unit* for *Twenty-First Century* problems.

*T*HE MULTIVERSE CONTAINS parallel Earths, many of which house unique versions of the Avengers. In one dimension, General Nick Fury, the head of S.H.I.E.L.D., is given the task of forming an Avengers team, the Ultimates. He hires Dr. Bruce Banner to recreate the lost Super-Soldier serum that created Captain America.

The Super-Agents

Fury believes that Earth faces a secret alien menace and the President authorizes a $150 billion project to create the Ultimates, a team of super-soldiers like Captain America who can safeguard the security of the planet. Fury recruits Tony Stark, creator of the Iron Man armor, Dr. Hank Pym, who is working on a formula to become Giant-Man, and his wife Janet, the Wasp.

BANNER BLOWS IT

Working out of a rundown research facility in Pittsburgh, Banner is disappointed when Fury refuses to allow him to conduct trials on civilians, so he tests his new formula upon himself. He is transformed into a monstrous Hulk and goes on a cross-country rampage. The rest of Fury's new Avengers team manage to subdue the Hulk and, after covering up Banner's connection to Hulk, Fury puts him back to work.

ARROWS OF DEATH

Hawkeye and Black Widow lead the assault on the office block, which seems to be staffed by ordinary workers. However the workers are really shape-shifting aliens plotting to take over the world.

The Alien Nest

While the public's attention is focused on the newly-formed Ultimates team, Clint "Hawkeye" Barton and Natasha "the Black Widow" Romanova run covert operations for Fury. The Widow and Hawkeye learn that the aliens are called the Chiaturi. Eight feet (2.4 meters) tall and reptilian in appearance, these aliens can assume human form. Before long, Black Widow and Hawkeye have targeted two adjacent office building which, according to information received, are fully staffed by potential alien invaders.

Hitler Was an Alien

Fury reveals that the Chiaturi threat to humanity is nothing new. In fact, the civilized world has already fought and defeated them once—during World War II, when the shape-shifting aliens infiltrated the Nazi party.

The Deadly Trap

Fury briefs the Ultimates on the Chiaturi menace and their recent attempt to contaminate the water supply with mind-controlling drugs. Sure that the aliens are preparing a global takeover, he launches a major offensive against them. However, the aliens have infiltrated S.H.I.E.L.D.'s psi-division and have been feeding Fury false information. Fury's forces are heading into a trap.

It was the psychics, wasn't it?

S.H.I.E.L.D. DESTROYED

Fury's troops are destroyed by a nuclear bomb. The Chiaturi then invade the Ultimates' Triskelion base and slaughter every S.H.I.E.L.D. agent on the premises.

THE POWER OF KLEISER

Leader of the Chiaturi, Kleiser possesses superhuman strength and the ability to heal from almost any injury.

Okay, Kleiser. Let's see what you got here, huh?

GAH!

Enemy From the Past

Saved from destruction by one of Iron Man's force-fields, Fury leads his troops to the new alien base where Captain America discovers Kleiser, an old enemy from World War II. With the aid of Thor, the Ultimates battle a fleet of Chiaturi starships, while Cap hits Kleiser with everything he's got; but the alien keeps coming back for more.

Hulk Smash!

Realizing that there's no other way to stop Kleiser, Cap calls in Banner and orders him to be thrown from a helicopter, knowing that he'll transform into the Hulk before he hits the ground. Not even Kleiser can withstand the full fury of an angry Hulk.

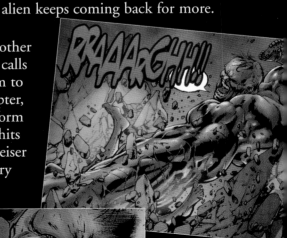

RRAAARGHH!!!

Well, my friend, it could appear that congratulations are in...

To prevent the alien creature from ever rising again, the Hulk tears it apart with his bare hands.

YOUNG AVENGERS

WHAT IF YOU COULD see yourself in ten years and hated the person you had become? In one possible future, Kang the Conqueror visited himself as a teenager and outlined the destiny awaiting him. Instead of being impressed, the young man was shocked and disgusted. He vowed to change his future by traveling back in time and enlisting the help of Kang's foes, the Avengers.

BLACK CAP
The formula that created Captain America was tested on some black soldiers. Eli's grandfather was the sole survivor.

YOUNG GUNS

When Kang found that the Avengers had disbanded, he formed his own team, consisting of spell-caster Billy "Asgardian" Kaplan, Eli "Patriot" Bradley, a young man with the super-soldier formula, and Teddy "Hulkling" Altman, a super-strong shape-shifter.

IRON LAD
The young Kang has neuro-kinetic armor that reacts to his thoughts.

GROWING PAINS
The team rescued a wedding party that was being held hostage at St. Patrick's Cathedral and later battled the Growing Man, who had been sent by Kang to retrieve his younger self. This robot burst into dozens of smaller robots that joined the attack.

New Recruits
Dubbed "The Young Avengers" by the press, the team picked up two more members: Cassie "Titan" Lang, daughter of the deceased Ant-Man who can grow to giant size, and Kate Bishop, a young weapons expert.

YOUR SALVATION HAS ARRIVED.

HOLY--!

A-AND IN A DRAMATIC DEVELOPMENT, THE CONTROVERSIAL SUPER-TEAM KNOWN AS THE THUNDERBOLTS HAS APPEARED AT THE SHOW!

BARON ZEMO...

Real Redemption

The Thunderbolts eventually decided that they wanted to reform. They turned against Baron Zemo and invited Hawkeye to lead them. He arranged for them to get full pardons for their crimes. As part of the deal, the Thunderbolts were forbidden to use their powers in public so the team temporarily disbanded. The team now includes Mach-IV, Songbird, Atlas, Blizzard, Captain Marvel, Speed Demon, Joystick, and Radioactive Man.

NEW INVADERS

*D*URING WORLD WAR II, Captain America, Bucky, the Sub-Mariner, the Human Torch and his partner Toro banded together to fight the Nazi menace. They were joined by other costumed crime-fighters like Spitfire, Union Jack and the Blazing Skull. With the rise of global terrorism, a secret government agency contacted U.S.Agent John Walker and commissioned him to assemble a team of superhuman anti-terrorists—a new team of Invaders.

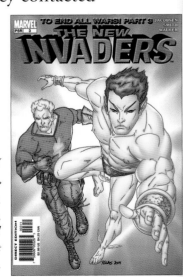

THE OLD AND THE NEW

Walker brought Spitfire and the Blazing Skull out of retirement. He also recruited a new Union Jack, Sub-Mariner, the Human Torch, and Tara, an android who burst into flame when exposed to oxygen.

THUNDERBOLTS

*T*HEY WERE A LIE that grew to become the truth. When the Avengers were apparently killed battling Onslaught, Baron Zemo sensed the public's need for new heroes. He outfitted his gang of criminals with new costumes and names and rechristened the team the Thunderbolts. The plan was to win support and then take over the world...

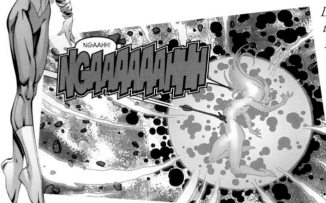

NGAAHH!

NGAAAAAHHH

During one of the team's attempts to save the world, Hawkeye was forced to destroy Moonstone, the woman he loved, when her powers went out of control.

Beyond borders, beneath the seas and behind enemy lines, the New Invaders hunted the terrorists that threatened the civilized world.

Afterword by Tom DeFalco

THE AVENGERS is actually the super-team title that Stan Lee was supposed to create at the beginning of the Marvel Universe, but he and Jack Kirby did the Fantastic Four instead. Martin Goodman, who owned the company that would eventually be known as Marvel Comics, was playing golf one day with some big shot from rival DC Comics. Goodman learned that DC's best-selling title was *The Justice League of America*, a team of super heroes, and immediately told Stan to come up with the same thing for Marvel. Well, the Justice League united all of DC's top heroes, but Marvel didn't have any suitable heroes at that precise moment. Stan probably could have resurrected Captain America, Sub-Mariner, and the original Human Torch—which he did later on—but he preferred to stretch his imagination and the boundaries of comics by creating the FF, a super-team for people who didn't like super-teams. When that title proved a success, he introduced more and more heroes until it seemed only natural to team them. Of course, Stan soon grew bored with the Avengers lineup and started changing the team.

If the Avengers can be summed up in a single word, it's "change." The team's membership changed with its second issue. A former member became an enemy with its third issue. A new member was added to the ranks in its fourth issue, and so on. In 2004, the entire structure of the Avengers was disassembled and replaced and that, too, is destined to change. If the Avengers teach us anything, it's that change is inevitable. We have to expect it and deal with it. A worthy lesson for children and adults alike!

Whenever I think of the Avengers, certain issues immediately spring to mind: *Avengers #4*, when Captain America burst on the scene… *Avengers #9*, the introduction and death of Wonder Man… *Avengers #17*, the old order changeth…and *Avengers #59* where I first learned that even an android can cry. I also think of Stan Lee and Jack Kirby who started the whole ball rolling and Roy Thomas and John Buscema, who took the team on the wildest rollercoaster rides. The Avengers were produced by a legion of truly talented creative people and I salute them all.

THE TIME HAS COME time has come for me to thank my editor, Alastair Dougall, for his exceptional patience and total support. The book may not have had all the angst and trauma of the last one, but life still did get a tad too interesting along the way.

I am also grateful to the talented Lisa Lanzarini who designed this book and keeps getting better with each new set of layouts.

While the original comics were my actual source material, I also relied rather heavily on the work of people like Mark Gruenwald, Peter Sanderson, Elliot Brown, Howard Mackie, Mark Bernardo, Bob Budiansky, Tom Brevoort, Eric Fein and all the others who contributed to *The Official Handbook of the Marvel Universe* (all three editions).

Anyone interested in the Avengers should also look in on the current monthly comic books— *New Avengers, Young Avengers, Ultimates* and, of course, *Iron Man,* and *Captain America*. The Avengers earlier adventures have been reprinted in a variety of formats, from the *Marvel Masterworks* to the *Essential Editions* and dozens of trade paperbacks.

This book is dedicated to Jimmy, Samantha. Bernie, Eddy, Tommy, Danielle, Christopher, Allison, Stephen, Meredith, Alexa, Andrew, Gerald, Carolyn, Ryan and the new addition we're expecting in November—they are my mightiest heroes and I thank them for helping me carry on and for giving me a reason to remain a storyteller. I would also like to express my gratitude to you, my reader, for just being there!

HOO-HA!

Tom D.

Gazetteer

Index

Main entries are in **bold**

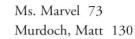

LONDON, NEW YORK, MUNICH,
MELBOURNE, AND DELHI

DK PUBLISHING, INC.

PROJECT EDITOR Alastair Dougall
SENIOR ART EDITOR & BRAND MANAGER Lisa Lanzarini
ASSOCIATE DESIGNERS Nick Avery, Jill Bunyan
PUBLISHING MANAGER Simon Beecroft
CATEGORY PUBLISHER Alex Allan
PRODUCTION Rochelle Talary
DTP DESIGN Lauren Egan

First American Edition, 2005, reprinted 2006, 2007
07 08 09 10 9 8 7 6 5 4 3
Published in the United States by DK Publishing, Inc.
375 Hudson Street, New York, New York 10016

DK Publishing, Inc. offers special discounts for bulk purchases for sales promotions or premiums.
Specific, large-quantity needs can be met with special editions, including personalized covers,
excerpts of existing guides, and corporate imprints. For more information, contact Special Markets
Department, DK Publishing, Inc., 375 Hudson Street, New York, NY 10014 Fax: 800-600-9098.

Published in Great Britain by Dorling Kindersley Limited.

Color reproduction by Media Development and Printing Ltd., UK

Printed and bound in China by Hung Hing.

Acknowledgments

DK Publishing would like to thank the following people:

Stan Lee for supplying the foreword; Ann Barrett for compiling the index;
Sarah E. Miller for editorial assistance; Mika Kean-Hammerson;
Blue Chip Illustration for the Avengers Mansion artwork.